TWICE IN A LIFETIME

It's been eighteen months since Anna's husband Finn died. Craving space to consider her next steps, she departs the city for the Cornish coast and the isolated Myrtle Cottage. But the best-laid plans often go awry, and when Anna's beloved dog Albie leads her away from solitude and into the path of Elliott, the owner of the nearby adventure centre, their lives become intertwined. As Anna's attraction to Elliott grows, so does her guilt at betraying Finn, until she remembers his favourite piece of advice: you only live once . . .

Books by Jo Bartlett
in the Linford Romance Library:

NO TIME FOR SECOND BEST
CHRISTMAS IN THE BAY
FALLING FOR DR. RIGHT
ST. FINBAR'S CROSS
ALWAYS THE BRIDESMAID
THE CHRISTMAS CHOIR
MURDER AT THE HIGHLAND
PRACTICE

JO BARTLETT

TWICE IN A LIFETIME

Complete and Unabridged

LINFORD
Leicester

First published in Great Britain in 2019

First Linford Edition
published 2020

A catalogue record for this book is available
from the British Library.

ISBN 978–1–4448–4513–6

Published by
Ulverscroft Limited
Anstey, Leicestershire
Set by Words & Graphics Ltd.
Anstey, Leicestershire
Printed and bound in Great Britain by
T. J. International Ltd., Padstow, Cornwall

This book is printed on acid-free paper

1

Maybe it had been a mistake to rent Myrtle Cottage. Even getting there was suddenly terrifying. It was just four walls, but it held so many memories of a time when life was good. Back then Anna had often willed something to happen, something to shake things up. Be careful what you wish for, they said. How true that had turned out to be.

The tide was closing in and, any minute now, the stretch of beach that provided the only access to the cottage would disappear beneath the waves. Anna eased the car off the concrete ramp and onto the sand. She was used to sitting bumper-to-bumper in traffic — a city driver, perfectly capable of racing for the last parking space and leaning heavily on the horn if someone cut her up — but this was different. Finn had always driven when they were

1

down here and somehow the twisting Cornish roads made her more nervous than London ever had.

Holding her breath as the tyres touched the sand, she half-expected them to start spinning, leaving her hopelessly stranded at the edge of the water. Only the car didn't stop, it glided effortlessly across the beach as though there'd been no change in the surface at all.

'Okay, Albie, we're going to make it.' She reached out a hand and a wet brown nose gave her a reassuring nudge. 'We'll be alright here, just the two of us, won't we?' Another nudge from the Labrador, curled up on the passenger seat beside her, was all the reassurance she needed.

*　*　*

Bringing the last bag in from the car, a shadow moved at the corner of Anna's eye and for a moment she could have sworn it was him — Finn — standing there in the room, laughing at their good fortune that the cottage should have become unexpectedly free, and for two whole months at that. It was just a trick of the light, of course, not something she could reach out and touch. Finn was gone and, even a year in, it still twisted her insides every time she forced herself to admit it.

'I don't suppose the bride thought it was good luck.' Anna spoke aloud, in part to Albie — who briefly acknowledged her with a raise of his soft golden head, before going back to sniffing the unfamiliar skirting board — and in part to the empty space where her husband's presence seemed to hang.

'Just imagine being in her shoes, jilted a fortnight before the wedding and a six-week honeymoon going to waste!' It was what the agent from the holiday company had told her when she'd inquired about the cottage on a whim, one wet Wednesday afternoon; when the longing to be somewhere she and Finn had spent so much time alone together had almost overwhelmed her. 'Poor girl.' The woman from Cornish

3

Gems, whose name was Gwen, had confided over the phone. 'Must be the worst thing that can happen to a woman, being jilted, don't you think?'

Anna had barely resisted the urge to put the woman straight, to tell her that there were far worse things that could happen than narrowly escaping a marriage to someone who clearly didn't love you anyway, but she didn't. She'd discovered in the months since Finn had been gone that most people didn't want to hear what you *really* had to say, even when they seemed to be asking.

'Sounds terrible.' Anna had given the expected reply instead, before moving the conversation on. 'Did you say it's available for six weeks?'

'Well, they're both teachers, you see.' Gwen was getting into her stride now, as if regaling a plot from a TV soap. 'She had it all planned, a romantic summer in Cornwall. And in Port Kara of all places — there's always the chance of bumping into a royal down there these days, you know! But she's going to the Canaries with her brides-maids instead and, if I can rent it out again, she won't lose the hefty deposit she's paid. I'm sure it would be a huge weight off her mind.'

'I'll take the whole six weeks.' The words had come out of Anna's mouth almost as if someone else had spoken them. She hadn't planned on going away for anything like as long as that. Although what was stopping her? She'd sold the restaurant and the one thing that didn't keep her awake at night was worrying about money. Finn had seen to that.

'That's amazing!' The excitement in Gwen's voice went flat as quickly as it had arrived. 'Although you do realise it's *completely* cut off to vehicles at high tide? All the other cottages in Port Kara rent out without even advertising them, since it became such a celebrity hotspot, but Myrtle Cottage . . . '

'I've stayed there before.' Anna crossed the fingers on her left hand as she spoke, praying that Gwen wouldn't demand as much of her life story as she clearly had the jilted bride's.

'Well that's fantastic then and it's free the middle two weeks of September at the moment, straight after your stay, if you wanted to make it a full two months?'

'In for a penny.' The brittle laugh caught in Anna's throat, her voice catching there, too, as she reeled off her credit card details before she could change her mind. Gwen hadn't questioned her further; just relieved, it seemed, that the poor jilted bride wouldn't suffer any more. Some people had all the luck.

* * *

Elliott loved the early evening during the summer months, especially when it coincided with high tide and the tourists had cleared the beach. It was as if he owned the whole world looking out to sea from the top of the cliff face. He'd finished with the guests for the day, done more than his fair share of coaxing and cajoling nervous townies to do something adventurous, to take advantage of the activities they'd paid a high price for, but which, more often than not, terrified them in practice. Now it was his turn for a bit of adventure. The cliffs on this part of the headland were too sheer for any of his guests to attempt — even those who were on a return visit and had long since caught the adrenaline bug.

The rocks beneath the cliff face at Dagger's Head rose up from the water like the jagged teeth of a giant, just waiting to impale their victim. Further to the left was a series of rocky out-crops, inaccessible on foot, as they were now interspersed with narrow gaps on the old coastal path that seemed to erode further with every turn of the tide. Only an Olympic long jumper could navigate the track now, and even then, they'd risk plunging onto the rocks below. It was what Elliott liked best about the climb down the rockface and along the old coastal path, before he made his way back up the cliff further along using grappling irons — the absolute certainty that he wouldn't be disturbed. It wasn't that he didn't enjoy company but, having spent all day being sociable, solitude definitely had its appeal.

When he saw her, he almost lost his footing.

He was so shocked at the sight of her navigating the crumbling pathway that, had he been the type to believe in all that, he might have thought she'd emerged from the sea itself. With her long blonde hair falling in soft waves below her shoulders and the appealing curve of her body evident even from this distance, there was definitely something of the mermaid about her. Still, the fact that she was wearing jeans and appeared to be chasing a sandy-coloured Labrador along the path put paid to that particular illusion. The reality was that she was in danger of slipping and there was nowhere to go but down, onto rocks that would cut her to ribbons, and a sea that was far crueller than it looked, even on a warm summer's evening. A light breeze carried her shout up to Elliott, who was already moving as swiftly as he could towards her. She must have been calling the dog; Alfie or Albie, he couldn't quite make it out. The animal would be much more sure-footed than her, though, and she was taking a stupid risk running to try and catch it.

He looked down just in time to see the dog leap over a gap in the old coastal path, its front paws landing squarely on the other side, but its back legs falling short for a moment and scrabbling against the loose surface beneath. Elliott held his breath but kept moving towards the mystery woman all the time. No matter how ridiculous it was, he had a horrible premonition she was going to try to follow the dog across. Her voice was clearer now, the Labrador's name was definitely Albie and she was almost screaming it, her distress undeniable.

For a few more seconds the dog's

back legs scrabbled desperately against the unstable surface, but somehow it managed to get enough momentum to safely get all four paws onto the path itself. Elliott finally released his breath and tried calling out to the woman below, to warn her not to follow the dog, whatever she did. He shouted, his voice bouncing off the rockface, but she didn't even look up.

She was calling Albie to come back across the gap in the pathway to her and, as he got closer still, he could make out her face — pale with terror. He knew what she was going to do, and he was powerless to stop it. She wouldn't respond to his shouts, or wait for him to get there and help, because she had no idea he was on his way. The dog, on the other side of the gap, gingerly approached the edge he'd just scrabbled over, looked down and turned around again, whining loudly so that Elliott could hear, even from thirty feet or so away.

He was so close; she must hear him

now. He shouted again, just a simple but meaningful 'No!' this time, but still she didn't look up. The dog clearly wasn't willing to come back across the gap, and Elliott tried desperately to get to the woman before she did something really stupid. It was as if they were both moving in slow motion: him descending down the last twenty feet or so of the rock towards the old coast path, and her stepping off the pathway to try and breach the gap to the dog. He didn't take his eyes off her, convinced that if he held her in his gaze, he could keep her safe until he got there, and he almost lost his own footing again because of it.

She stepped off, when he was so close it felt as though he could almost have reached out and stopped her, but he was still about ten feet away. He heard the scream, close enough now to see the terror flicker in her bluey-green eyes, almost the exact colour of the waves crashing against the rocks below her. He was sure she was going to disappear into the gap, and he'd have to watch her fall, live with that on his conscience forever — that he hadn't been quick enough, couldn't save her. But, somehow, she managed to grab hold of something, an old tree root or maybe a large tuft of reed — although how long it would hold her weight was anyone's guess.

'Don't move, not even to look up at me, it might be enough to break whatever it is you're holding on to.' He was just above her now, on the rockface. He might have enjoyed the adrenaline surge of the fast-paced free climb down the cliff in other circumstances. The sort of risk his old friends would insist he only took because he missed the thrill of the chase since quitting London and his highly pressured job as a city financier, which showed just how little they really knew him. Not today though. Putting his own life in danger was one thing: he was an expert and it was always a carefully measured risk, just enough to make things interesting. Watching someone else do it, and totally recklessly too, was anything but fun.

'I don't think I can hold on anymore.' Her voice was small, as if even talking was an effort.

'You can do it, just a few more seconds. Don't talk, though, just hold on.'

Taking a grappling iron out of his rucksack, he secured it as swiftly as he could, trying to keep calm as he threaded the climbing rope through it, able now to make out the panicked breathing of the woman just below him and the whining of the dog on the ledge to his left.

Securing the rope around his waist, he reached down, grabbing her wrist. 'You're going to need to let go of what you're holding on to now and trust me.'

'I'm scared.' As she spoke, their eyes met properly for the first time, the fear there so obvious she didn't need the words.

'I know, but I promise you're going to be okay; I've got you now. What's your name?'

'Anna. Anna Turner.'

'Okay, Anna. We're going to do this; you can trust me. There's no way I'll let anything happen to you.' He'd keep hold of her or die trying. Slowly, she uncurled her fingers from what he could now see was a thick clump of reed roots. Someone must have been watching out for her — for that to hold her, and for Elliott to be in the right place at just the moment she'd decided to do something as crazy as she had. It wasn't her time and he'd make sure of it. 'That's it, now lift up your left arm too, so I can take hold of your other wrist.'

'Thank you.' When he looked into her eyes this time, there was something else there, something unreadable. Whatever it was, there was real sadness, and for the first time he wondered if she'd risked her life on purpose. Surely no one would do something that crazy without some sort of death wish.

'Is Albie okay?' Her eyes darted towards the dog, flat against the cliff face, still whining.

'He's fine. Let me get you to the safe

part of the path first and then we'll worry about the dog. I'm Elliott, by the way.' He laughed then, at the absurdity of their introduction, glad to break the tension. The intensity of the look in her eyes had been too much to take. Added to which, the heady smell of her perfume, at close proximity, was having an entirely inappropriate effect on him.

* * *

Anna had never been so glad to feel the stability of the ground beneath her feet, as Elliott manoeuvred them both onto the safe side of the path, which Albie had leapt from. She thanked whatever it was — fate, pure good luck or something else — that had put him on the cliff face, at just the moment she'd decided to do something so ridiculous.

Her decision-making had hardly been rational since she'd lost Finn, and Albie was all that she had left of him — he'd been their baby, whilst they waited until they were ready to have one of their own, never knowing that time would run out first — so she couldn't lose him too. Yet, despite the sheer torture of the months since Finn's death and the times she'd wished she could join him, dangling over that ledge she'd been sure of one thing — she wanted to live, even without the husband she'd lost far too soon.

'Thank you.' The words seemed inadequate for what he'd done, but she couldn't help asking for more. 'Albie . . . '

'It's okay, I'm going for him now.' Elliott gave her a reassuring smile, his deep brown eyes crinkling slightly in the corners as he did. He made a pretty good hero. He definitely looked the part — the classic tall, dark and handsome, not that she noticed those things anymore — and she'd been more than grateful of those powerful arms hauling her up and out of danger. She doubted he'd have been able to do it if Finn had been alive; she'd eaten far too well back then and running a restaurant together had put temptation in her path. But eating, like most things, had lost its appeal without Finn and now she was far too thin according to her well-meaning parents. Ironically, it had probably saved her life, in a roundabout way. Although there was no denying it was Elliott who was really responsible for that.

'Thanks. I know it's a lot to ask when you've already rescued me, but daft as it seems, that disobedient dog means the world to me.'

'It's not daft at all. Trying to leap across a gap that big,' Elliott paused and looked into the water below them, 'now that's daft. Although I'd probably choose a much stronger expression than that.'

Before she had a chance to reply, he began to climb back up the rockface, crossing the gap she'd tried to breach a few feet above where she was standing. He looked like a professional, with all the right gear for climbing, and she knew Albie was in safe hands.

Like most Labradors, Albie was friendly and would usually do anything for a treat, but his experience in the last twenty minutes or so had clearly brought out the coward in him and he almost shrank into the cliffside as Elliott strapped some sort of harness on to him. Albie barked in protest as his rescuer hoisted him upwards, his legs paddling in thin air like a character from a cartoon.

Once Anna started to laugh, she couldn't stop. Relief, shock and a whole gamut of emotions, which sat far too close to the surface these days, threatened to overwhelm her.

'Are you okay?' Elliott placed a hand on her arm. All she could do was nod, through a mix of tears and laughter, as he picked up the lead she'd dropped, when she'd tried to follow Albie, and clipped it onto the dog's collar before taking off the harness. 'I'm not taking any chances with Houdini here.'

'That's probably a wise move. I think being out of the city for once just went to his head, to *both* of our heads. I should never have let him off or taken this path. It's just so different from when we were last here.' A look of relief swept across his face as she spoke.

'I did wonder if you were . . . ' He paused for a second. 'Sorry, now I'm the one being stupid. It's not as if you'd take a dog with you if you were planning to jump, is it?' He had a disarming smile and his accent wasn't typically local, although the even tan and the blond tips to his otherwise dark hair meant he wouldn't have looked out of place striding into the surf. She shook her head at the thought; surfing was Finn's first love and if she wanted to pretend to Elliott that everything was okay, she had to keep thoughts of her husband at least partially at bay.

'No, I definitely wasn't planning on it. Not with the price I've paid to rent Myrtle Cottage for the whole summer. It would be a real waste to end it all on day one.' She laughed a bit too hard at the feeble joke, but Elliott smiled again, patting Albie's head as he nudged at his rescuer's legs.

19

'It's a quaint little place. A bit lonely perhaps, when the tide cuts it off, but it's a honeymooner's paradise.' His eyes flickered towards her left hand, where her wedding and engagement rings still sat, allowing her to keep up the pretence that she still had Finn.

'I'm not on honeymoon, I'm . . . ' She'd been about to use the dreaded word *widowed*, but she didn't want to see that look on his face; that mixture of pity and embarrassment everyone seemed to get at the mention of it. Being widowed at twenty-eight somehow made other people really uncomfortable. 'It's just me and Albie. That's why I had to rescue him, I'm never lonely with him about.' The tears that stung her eyes were unexpected, but Elliott really had no idea what he had done for her.

'I'd say it's nice to meet you, Anna, but I'm not sure that's the right thing to say, given the circumstances. Are you okay to get back down to the cottage by yourself, or do you want me to walk with you?'

'We'll be fine, because of you. I'm sorry to have interrupted your climb, but so thankful to whatever it was that put you here tonight. What are the odds of an expert climber being on hand, just when you need one?' She laughed again, thankful that he hadn't questioned her further about being on her own; she wasn't sure she was up to explaining what had happened to Finn.

'With me, the odds are pretty good around here. I own an adventure centre, up on the clifftop and this is the sort of thing I do for relaxation.' It was his turn to laugh, in response to the expression she knew must have crossed her face. 'It's no problem, just promise me you won't try anything like that again. If it's been a while since you stayed, the old coastal path has been really damaged over the past year or so and there's none of it that's really safe anymore.'

'I promise, but if there's ever anything I can do to pay you back, just say the word.' She kissed his cheek, the warmth and slight tang of salt on his skin stirring another memory.

'I'm just glad you're both alright. Stay safe, okay?' Elliott lit up the fading light with one last killer smile. 'And maybe head up to Dorton's Adventure Centre whilst you're here, so you can learn about the coastal paths that *are* safe to follow, and what to do when you get into trouble? At least that way I'll be able to sleep at night!'

'I might just take you up on that.' Anna watched as he raised a hand in response, already heading back up the cliff-side. He was definitely a pro.

The walk back down to the cottage was blissfully uneventful and even the irrepressibly excitable Albie was subdued. Despite her assurance to Elliott that she and Albie would never be lonely, the quiet back inside Myrtle Cottage was painful. It was probably just the drama of almost plunging between the cliffs into the sea but closing her eyes — with Albie's head on her feet as she sunk into an armchair

— the usual visions of Finn were interspersed with Elliott's smile and a new emotion bubbled to the surface. Guilt.

2

The screeching of a seagull woke Anna just after eight a.m. It would have seemed absurdly late back in the days when she'd run the restaurant, rising at five a.m. and heading to the markets at least three times a week to pick up fresh produce. Back then, sleeplessness had never been something that had plagued her. The long hours spent on her feet and frenetic pace of running one of the most successful restaurants in London had been enough to ward off insomnia. There'd always been Finn's solid back to cuddle into, too — a safe haven even on the occasional night when she was worried about something stupid, like getting their tax returns in on time. All those sorts of worries seemed so trivial, now that Finn was gone.

Stretching, Anna forced herself to throw back the covers. Albie, who'd been lying on a rug by the side of her bed, got to his feet, his thick-set tail thudding against the wall of the bedroom.

'Sorry, boy, I bet you're desperate for a walk and your breakfast, aren't you?' He looked up at her, total trust in his eyes — he needed her as much as she needed him. 'I'll let you out for a bit and then we can have a proper walk after breakfast.' Was it insane to talk to a dog quite as often as she talked to Albie? It was hard luck if it was, they were a team now. The one solid presence left in her world.

★   ★   ★

'Morning.' She'd barely stepped outside the door of the cottage, with Albie on his lead, when another dog walker raised his hand in greeting and called out. She waved and nodded in response, dipping her head before he could strike up a conversation. It was strange how friendly dog walkers were; even in London where people were usually head down and hell-bent on getting to their own destination, it completely changed when you had a dog with you. She'd had conversations walking Albie on Hampstead Heath, where some of the other dog walkers had revealed more about their personal lives than she knew about some of her closest friends. But Anna always kept her head down these days.

Despite a cloudless sky, the wind was strong enough to whip up the surf and there were already a few wetsuit-clad surfers heading out with their boards; how long would it take before she stopped expecting one of them to be Finn?

'Come on, Alb, let's head into town and see if there's a market on today.' She missed so much of her old life, even the mixture of pressure and excitement that came from cooking for a restaurant full of diners with sky-high expectations. It was nothing like the wrenching emptiness of missing Finn, but it had all been tied up with their life together. Coming back to Cornwall was about letting go of the things that she'd been clinging to for the eighteen months since his death. She hadn't been able to go on holiday, or do the job she'd loved for so long, without him by her side. She'd barely been able to function at first, and happiness was a memory she couldn't quite conjure up anymore — like chasing a rainbow that just kept moving farther away.

There was magic in Port Kara, though, and watching Albie bounce along the edge of the shoreline, where the dying waves finally broke and turned over, she felt alive. It wasn't happiness, exactly, but it was the closest she'd felt to it for a long time.

Careful to stick to the well-signposted new coastal path after Elliott's warnings from the day before, Anna caught her breath as a couple about her age, walking towards her, stopped to kiss. Stepping back, the man pushed a strand of hair away from his companion's face. Did they realise how lucky they were, in that moment, when everything in their world was right? Anna hadn't, not until it was far too late. They didn't speak as she passed by, not even to offer a good morning, too engrossed in each other to notice the woman with tears in her eyes.

Making their way down to the harbour, Anna's mood seemed to lift again. The charming, hilly streets of Port Kara leading them to their destination were weaving their spell, just as they always had. She had to expect ups and downs, everyone had told her that. But being back in Port Kara made it seem possible that, one day, the ups would finally outweigh the downs again.

Just as she was drawing level with one of the wooden jetties that abutted the harbour wall, a boat chugged in to moor. There were a group of men and women on board, all of them wearing wet suits. There was a big pile of diving equipment on one side of the deck.

'Well, I must say, it's a relief to see you sticking to the safety of the harbour this morning. No more cliff-jumping for you and Albie!' She recognised Elliott's voice, even before she looked up. She tried to keep her focus firmly on his face and not the way the wetsuit clung to his body.

'Doing that once is a mistake anyone could have made. Doing it twice would be foolish.' She returned his smile, despite a twinge of annoyance that he'd brought her stupid mistake up again. Although, seeing as she and Albie owed him their lives, this was no time to hold a grudge. 'Looks like you were out diving early this morning?'

'The forecast said the wind was going to pick up, so I knew we'd get the best of the weather that way. Some of this lot haven't quite found their sea legs yet, and, even in the better weather, the journey back to Port Kara was a bit rough for one or two of them.'

'Not everyone's an action hero.'

'Are you making fun of me, Ms Turner?' He smiled more broadly this time, revealing perfectly even teeth. The fact that he'd remembered her name pleased her more than it should. He ran adventure holidays for a living, so he was probably used to learning the names of whole groups of people within minutes of meeting them. It didn't mean anything, and she shouldn't want it to.

'I just meant that not everyone has your physical abilities.' Her words were coming out all wrong. Why hadn't she just rushed past the boat, instead of stopping to speak to a man who made her feel safe and uncomfortable, all at the same time?

'Well, I'll take that as a compliment, I think.' Elliott grinned again, finding her ability to tie herself up in knots far too amusing for her liking. 'How about you? Can I interest you in a diving trip later in the week?'

'No way! I always stuck to dry land when my husband hit the surf; he couldn't even persuade me to try bodyboarding, let alone diving. There's something about the sea that's always scared me, even before . . . '

'Before what?' He was waiting for her to finish a sentence she'd never intended to start, the group around him beginning to gather up their stuff and get off the boat, whilst he kept his eyes firmly fixed on her. She had to say something or he might just stand there, staring at her all day. She'd never been good at making things up on the spot, anyway, so she might as well get it over with.

'My husband, Finn, had a surfing accident. He'd gone away with some friends to surf in South Africa for a week.' There was something about Elliott that made her say things she'd rather not have said. Maybe it was the way he went quiet, waiting for a response, until she was desperate to fill the silence. 'He'd always wanted to go, and I bought him the trip for his thirtieth birthday, otherwise he'd never have been there.' She dug her nails into the palms of her hands — going down that path again would kill her too; it had taken months of counselling to stop her fixating on *what if*s.

'You don't need to tell me if you don't want to.' Elliott's voice was reassuring, the way it had been on the cliff the night before, when he'd promised he wouldn't let her fall.

'It's okay.' For some reason she wanted to tell him. He clearly thought she was reckless, after the way she'd acted the night before, but maybe this would help him understand. 'Finn was out surfing early in the morning with two of his friends. I'd made him promise he wouldn't take any stupid risks, like going out surfing by himself.'

Elliott had moved closer to her as the skipper tied the back of the boat to the mooring post. The rest of the guests and crew were already getting drinks from a wooden kiosk to the right of where she stood, their laughter intermittently rising with the breeze that was still picking up pace. Elliott probably couldn't wait to get away, he had guests to get back to after all, and here she was wittering on. She should just say it, blurt it out, tell this stranger who'd saved her life just how much she wished he'd been around when her husband had needed the same sort of help, and nobody had been around to provide it.

'He kept his promise, not to take the risks we'd talked about. The waves weren't even that big, he'd surfed in much rougher seas, but he was knocked off his board and hit his head on a rock just below the surface of the water that none of them had known was there. It was a minute or two before his friends realised he hadn't resurfaced, but as soon as they did they got him back to the beach. They tried CPR, the lifeguards did too, for twenty minutes until the paramedics reached him, but it was too late.'

'Oh no, I'm so sorry. And here I am running my mouth off about you coming diving. I never did know when to shut up.'

'It's not your fault, how were you supposed to know? I can't expect to avoid every mention of the sea, especially not in a place like Port Kara.'

'It does seem an odd choice to come to a surfer's paradise.' He shook his head. 'I'm sorry. Shall I take my size ten feet out of my mouth and just disappear? It's none of my business why you wanted to come here.'

'It was our go-to place whenever we managed a few days off.' She smiled at the memory. It hadn't been nearly as often as she'd wanted it to be. Running the restaurant had meant they'd had to take a lot of holidays separately, but at least they'd made the time they had together count. It was one of the things she'd always been grateful for, having such a good team at the restaurant, so they'd managed to snatch *some* time alone. She wouldn't have made it through the past eighteen months if she hadn't had that thought to cling on to; without it she'd have drowned, just like Finn. 'I used to walk Albie for miles, then sit and paint, whilst Finn surfed. But we'd spend the rest of the time together, not doing much at all. Just being together was enough, do you know what I mean?'

'I can guess, but I've never had that sort of relationship.'

'I find that hard to believe.'

'That, I'll definitely take as a compliment.' He smiled again, making it even harder to believe someone like him had never been in love. With his dark hair pushed away from his forehead and those dark eyes which never seemed to leave your face, there must have been plenty of women in Port Kara lining up to change that. The action hero bit probably appealed to most of them too. But not her, not any more. Even if her heart hadn't been shattered into a million tiny pieces that she had no idea how to put back together, she couldn't have fallen for someone like Elliott. Someone who got his kicks — and made his living — from chasing an adrenaline rush. If she ever worked out how to let herself feel anything for another man, she was going to choose someone safe and steady. That person would never hold as much of her heart in his hands as Finn had — she didn't want to risk that again — but at least her patchwork heart would keep beating that way.

'Good, because it was meant as a compliment. Thanks for listening, and thanks again for last night, but I'd better get going.' She smiled as a pretty redhead standing by the kiosk called out Elliott's name for the third time. 'In fact, I think your public are getting impatient.'

'What are your plans for the day, if you aren't venturing on to the beach?' Elliott clearly wasn't in any hurry to respond to the woman calling his name. He'd just held up his hand and given her a nod, indicating that he'd be there in a minute. Once upon a time, Anna might have been flattered that he'd rather talk to her, but she was still Finn's.

'Albie and I were just going to have a wander around Port Kara to familiarise ourselves with the place again and see what else has changed since our last visit. Apart from the old coastal path disappearing, of course.' The roots of her hair prickled at the memory of how stupid she'd been, and how close she'd come to losing Albie as a result.

'How long has it been since you were last here?'

'Two years.' It might as well have been a lifetime.

'Well, there's definitely somewhere you need to check out then. Port Kara won an international award last year for the fish market which opened at the west end of the harbour. The scallops are the freshest you'll ever taste, and I guarantee you won't be disappointed; if you like seafood, that is?'

'Are you on commission?' Anna raised her eyebrows, glad they were back on safe ground. Food was one thing she could *always* talk about.

'Not at all, although the way my chef spends money there, I think I should probably get some shares in the business.' Elliott finally stepped off the boat and fell into an easy stride beside her, as they drew level with the kiosk where his guests were still waiting. He patted the shoulder of another man standing on the edge of the group. 'Great dive, everyone; there should be some really good footage on the Go Pro when we get back to the centre. I'll leave you in Greg's capable hands, I'm just going to take my friend Anna up to the market and show her around.'

'You don't have to.' Anna had no intention of going anywhere with Elliott, and she hadn't missed the daggered look the redhead had thrown in her direction. 'Anyway, what am I going to do with Albie? I couldn't be responsible for what he might do if he got within two hundred metres of a stall of fresh fish. You've seen how he can jump.'

'I have indeed.' Elliott bent down to stroke the dog's head. 'And we definitely don't want a repeat of that. You could tie him up outside, though.'

'I couldn't risk it.' Anna's voice cracked and the redhead shot her another dismissive look. She couldn't expect other people to understand just how precious Albie was, and that she'd truthfully rather die than have anything happen to him. Elliott already knew it, though.

'Of course not.' He squeezed her hand and something in her chest fluttered, something else she desperately didn't want to feel. 'We'll only be ten minutes, though, and Greg can keep an eye on Albie for you, just while we have a quick look around.'

'I couldn't ask him to do that.' She didn't want to, either.

'Greg's my right hand man.' Elliott clapped a hand on the other man's shoulder again. 'You'll guard Albie with your life, won't you, mate?'

'My pleasure.' Greg looked Anna up and down as he spoke, a slow smile spreading over his face. He'd obviously jumped to completely the wrong conclusion about her and Elliott, and it made her want to bolt all the more. Greg had it wrong, but just the look on his face made her feel like she was cheating on Finn.

'So, that's a deal then?' Elliott was watching her again and she found herself nodding, even though she'd fully intended to say no. Handing Albie's lead to Greg, she followed Elliott along the harbour side, as if some force beyond her control had made the decision for her.

★ ★ ★

Elliott had been only too aware of the way Janey Summers had looked at him and it was clear she'd set her sights on him from the moment she'd arrived at the adventure centre. Glaston's, the insurance firm she worked for, were a potentially very lucrative corporate client to land, and they could bring a lot of business to the centre, organising adventure weekends and team-building sessions for their staff. Any other time he probably wouldn't have fought Janey's advances all that hard. She was a good-looking woman, but not the sort he'd want in his life on a long-term basis — she had too few soft edges for that.

He'd heard her screaming at her PA about something over breakfast; the poor bloke had looked as if he wanted the ground to open up and swallow him. He'd seen that sort of bullying too many times before, passed off under the guise of being tough in business. His father, Charles, was a master at it, and he'd made it all too clear that Elliott's desire to be nothing like him was one of his biggest failures. Although, in the end, his failures had been too numerous to count, according to Charles Dorton.

Elliott had lived a lie for far too long but, despite what his father thought, he'd made more money in fifteen years than most people make in a lifetime. Sinking it all into Dorton's Adventure Centre might have been idiotic in his father's eyes, but he was a million times happier in Cornwall than he'd ever been in London. Turning his back on the potential of earning a seven-figure salary had been easy when it meant saying goodbye to so many phoney people too. It had been a dog-eat-dog world, and most of his colleagues would have happily stabbed him in the back to get one over on him in a business deal. There wasn't enough money in the world to persuade him to go back to following in his father's corporate footsteps, so Janey Summers definitely wasn't his type.

Not that the lack of any long-term prospect was a problem; that was the last thing Elliott wanted anyway. Which meant he'd probably have met Janey for the drink she'd suggested later — if it hadn't been for Anna. Maybe it was the way those big bluey-green eyes of hers filled with tears every so often, or the way she tried so hard to hold them back. Whatever it was, he couldn't ignore it, and Janey might as well have been invisible for all he'd noticed her once Anna had arrived. But he didn't need to see Janey's face to know she wouldn't be pleased. She was obviously used to getting what she wanted, but if he lost the Glaston's contract because he'd rather spend half an hour with Anna, than a night with Janey, then that's the way it would have to be. His father would probably call him an idiot for that, too.

'You don't have to babysit me, you know. I don't make a habit of needing my life saved and I'm pretty sure I can find the fish market all on my own.' Anna narrowed her eyes as she spoke and set her shoulders back. Even pulling herself up to her full height, she couldn't have been more than five feet four. If he'd called her cute, she'd probably have pushed him into the harbour, though. Something gave him the feeling she resented showing any vulnerability, but she hadn't been able to hide it in the conversations they'd had so far.

'Maybe I'm the one who could use the company.' He brushed off her comment. She might not want his help, but she was going to get it anyway. 'What sort of job have you got that lets you stay down here for a whole month in the summer? Are you a teacher?'

'No, I'm retired.' She laughed as he widened his eyes. 'That's not strictly true; maybe taking a belated gap year is more like it. My husband and I ran a business, and I've recently sold it on, which means I've got the time and the money to decide what I want to do next.'

'What sort of business were you in?'

'Um, you know, just a . . . catering firm.' Her hesitation was obvious, but he wasn't going to push her for more information; if she wanted to tell him, she would.

'With that sort of background, I'm sure you're going to love the market here. There's a fantastic farmers' market on Fridays, too.' He reeled off the patter he knew by heart, the sort of

44

information that was plastered all over the Dorton Adventure Centre website; after all, even adrenaline junkies had to eat, and it was the centre's growing reputation for great food and high-end accommodation that was helping to set it apart from other similar centres dotted all over the country. Port Kara was attracting its share of high-profile celebrity holidaymakers too, and rumour had it that some of the younger members of the royal family had stayed for a few days surfing at the start of the season. Everyone was upping their game as a result, and Elliott wasn't about to be left behind.

'It'll make a change to cook for pleasure instead of demanding customers.' She smiled as she spoke, and there was that pull again, the undeniable attraction that had stirred inside him, even when he'd been racing down the cliffside to pull her to safety. It would be much easier to choose who you were attracted to — someone like Anna had far too much emotional baggage for the sort of casual relationship he was after. The adventure centre took ninety percent of everything he had to give, and Anna wasn't a ten percent sort of woman. His parents' bitter divorce had taught him only too well what happened if you tried to have a relationship that wasn't your number one priority. He was more like his mother, which was something else his father told him every time he got the chance. Mary Dorton was a dreamer, according to her ex-husband. She'd poured her heart and soul into the art shop she ran in the Sussex countryside, whilst his father had been working twelve-hour days in London, and then wining and dining clients late into the evening. They'd grown so far apart that the divorce had been inevitable; but the mudslinging and blame that had come with it could have been avoided if they'd retained the ability to see even a fraction of the other person's point of view. Now they could barely stand to be in the same county, never mind the same room. If

Elliott ever did find someone to share his life with, it would have to be someone who shared his dreams too, and who was prepared to make the adventure centre their number one priority. He had more chance of winning the lottery, and he didn't even buy a ticket.

'So will you have anyone to cook for whilst you're staying at Myrtle Cottage? You must be expecting some visitors if you're down here for so long?'

'I'm not sure I should be telling you whether I'm planning to be in the cottage all by myself.' She put her head on one side, as if she was trying to work out his motivation for asking. But he wasn't even sure himself.

'I promise I'm not an axe murderer, and I won't tell anyone else you're out there by yourself either.' Port Kara was probably one of the safest places in the world, but it was still a long time for her to be on her own, cut off from the rest of the world once the tide rose up.

'I know you won't. And to answer

your question, I'm not expecting anyone to come and visit. In fact, hardly anyone knows where I am.' She jerked her head back. 'I probably shouldn't say that, either! It's just as well I trust you. I think saving my life puts you on that footing, don't you? I came down here to get away from everything, and, if I see friends, they'll want to talk about Finn, and ask how I am all the time. Sometimes I just want to *be*. Does that sound crazy?'

'Funnily enough, I know exactly what you mean.' Anna wasn't the only one who'd run away, but she didn't need to hear what had brought him to Port Kara. Escaping from a lifestyle he hated would sound so unimportant compared to what she'd been through. 'What about your family — they're not always so easy to shake off, are they?'

'Mum and Dad live out in Portugal and I've promised to spend a month out there when my lease of Myrtle Cottage comes to an end. It took a bit of persuading to convince them that I'd be okay on my own. I won't be telling them anything about the little incident on the cliff, put it that way.'

'I get that too, parents can be . . . tricky. But I'm sure you'll find something delicious at the market, even if you're only cooking for one.' He stopped outside a large single-storey building, clad with black wood that made it look like an old barn. 'This is where all the fresh fish is brought in daily. First thing in the morning, you get traders turn up down here from as far away as London, bidding on stock for the restaurants up there.'

'I don't think I've ever been to a market so close to the source of its produce before.' There was a look of genuine excitement on her face. She might have been downplaying the catering business, but she'd obviously been passionate about it once upon a time.

'Shall we go inside?'

'You don't have to spend all your time with me. I think even I can take it from here, unless there's a treacherous pathway inside that I know nothing about?'

'It's perfectly safe, but I'd like to come with you, if you don't mind?' There was no reason to, she was right, but the adventure centre gave him the perfect excuse. 'My chef asked me to check whether there's been a new catch of langoustine. We've got a gala dinner tomorrow night and he needs to plan the menu.'

'So you manage the adventure centre?'

'Yes.' He hesitated for a moment, not sure whether to tell her that the business was all his or not. It had set him back over two million pounds and he'd seen some people's attitudes change when they realised he wasn't just the hired help. But Anna didn't seem like she'd care either way. Fifteen years as a city trader had sucked his soul dry and the type of people who were impressed by the fact that he owned the centre were just as draining.

'I bought the adventure centre when I stopped working in London. I wanted a real chef to run the restaurant, so we could offer our guests food that's as wonderful as the setting. Only I hadn't banked on quite how temperamental the chef I appointed would be. Any treacherous coastal path you might find would still be easier to navigate than negotiating with Carmelo.'

'Ah, yes, I remember those sorts of working relationships well.' She smiled again, and it was like the sun had come out, even inside the market hall.

'Did you do the cooking for your business yourself?'

'Sometimes I cooked, but quite often I was the assistant chef. I suppose you'd call me a sous chef, if you wanted to use the correct term, but all of us worked as a team and desserts were my speciality.'

'And was your husband hands-on in the business too?'

'He was the driving force and he'd have been in his element in a place like this.' She stopped to look at some lobsters sitting on a bed of ice on one of the stalls. 'It's hard to look at anything food-related and not think about what Finn's opinion would have been.'

'Maybe I shouldn't have brought you here.' He'd more or less forced her to come but upsetting her again was the last thing he wanted.

'It's fine. I can think about him now without completely dissolving. Well most of the time, anyway.'

They wandered between the stalls in easy silence, Elliott enjoying the opportunity to watch Anna interacting with the stallholders. Whatever her role in the business had been, she was a good negotiator, haggling for prices, and clearly more than capable of telling the best produce from anything of not quite such good quality.

'Elliott!' There was only one person who shouted his name in quite that way, demanding instant attention — Carmelo. The fact that his chef had taken it upon himself to head down to the fish market wasn't a good sign. He only ever did that sort of thing when there was a problem at the restaurant, and he'd made it quite clear that purchasing the produce was beneath him. He was an artist — he'd told Elliott as much — there to create, not to haggle over the price of the daily catch.

'What are you doing here? I thought you trusted Sara to take care of all of the ordering now?' Elliott had a horrible feeling he knew what was coming.

'She has gone. She walk out of the restaurant and say she don't want to work with me no more!' Carmelo threw up his hands, as if the sous chef's disappearance had absolutely nothing to do with him.

'Do I need to ask why?'

'I was just talking to one of the waitresses, Darcy. Sara go crazy for no reason.' Carmelo was doing his best to look like the wounded party.

'*Talking*?' Elliott shook his head. If Carmelo's track record was anything to go by, he'd have moved far more quickly with the young waitress than that. Poor Sara, she'd had no idea Carmelo valued her more as a sous chef than a girlfriend. Elliott was going to have to put his foot down this time, though; they couldn't afford to keep losing staff at the rate they were. Carmelo had already cost him a great bar manager, who'd also had her heart broken, and the services of a cleaning company. They'd run out of options in a place like Port Kara if Carmelo didn't slow down.

'Sara take life too seriously.' Carmelo gave a dismissive shrug. 'But I can't do everything!'

'Maybe you should have thought of that.' Elliott wasn't going to have it out with him in the market, especially not in front of Anna. But when they got back to the centre, he'd be straight with Carmelo. Artist or not, he couldn't keep treating people the way he did, not whilst they were working for Elliott, anyway.

'How you going to sort it?' Carmelo's cropped English was no doubt part of his charm when he was telling the women he met that they were the most beautiful he'd ever seen. But right now, it was getting on Elliott's nerves, especially as it made it sound like he was ordering Elliott to sort something out.

'Where do you expect me to magic up a replacement sous chef from, without any warning?' Elliott struggled to keep his tone level, but Carmelo had already lost interest, his gaze drifting towards where Anna stood quietly by Elliott's side.

'Use an agency.' Carmelo didn't look at him. He was looking Anna up and down in a very obvious way instead.

'It's the busiest time of the year; everyone who's in catering and who's good at their job will already be employed. We'll be lucky to get anyone at all, let alone anyone as good at their job as Sara.' Elliott's jaw muscles tightened. Carmelo was still staring at

Anna, and he had a sudden urge to land a punch square on his chef's nose. 'Will you at least look at me, while I'm trying to sort out the mess that you've made? Yet again.'

'Relax, I just see something so beautiful it make it difficult to concentrate. Women like Sara can be replaced, but others, they different.' Carmelo looked briefly at Elliott, before fixing his gaze firmly back on Anna. Did anyone really fall for that sort of rubbish? Judging by the look on Anna's face, she wasn't impressed — a mixture of amusement and irritation seemed to sum it up. Either way, Elliott had had enough

'I didn't want to do this here, Carmelo, but seeing as you don't seem to be able to take anything seriously, I'm telling you now that *this is serious*. If you can't stop mixing your personal life with your professional life, and rein in your outbursts, then I'm going to be asking you to follow Sara's lead and leave.' Elliott was vaguely aware that the activity around them seemed to have stopped. Shoppers and stallholders alike all wanted to listen to the drama unfolding in front of them. The urge just to punch Carmelo wasn't lessened by the smirk that had appeared on his face.

'You can't do without me. You all talk!' He'd got his chef's attention at least; Carmelo had finally dragged his eyes away from Anna.

'Oh, I think I'd manage just fine.' He was on a roll now. Months of having to manage Carmelo's histrionics had strained their relationship, but there was more to it than that — Anna deserved respect, she'd been through enough. The other women his chef had set his sights on did too and, whatever Carmelo might think, Sara was too much of an asset to lose.

'You seriously think you manage without me?' Carmelo's derisory laugh set the seal on it. It was madness when the adventure centre was full of guests, and it was the height of the season, but Elliott wasn't backing down.

'I think we'll manage much better

without you. Maybe I can even persuade Sara to come back and take over from you.' He was more or less banking on it.

'Ha, she nowhere near as good as me and you get everything you deserve!' Carmelo drew back a fist and his hand shot forward, but Elliott was far too fast for him. Grabbing the chef's wrist, he twisted his arm behind his back, almost lifting him off his feet in the process. Anna's gasp was audible.

'And so will you, Carmelo. Now, I want you to go back and pack up your stuff and be gone before I get back to the centre.' Elliott kept hold of the other man, even as Carmelo tried to make another move to lash out at him, this time with his foot. 'And if you try anything else, I've got a market full of witnesses here who'll testify that you tried to hit me, and a centre full of staff who'll back me up on your behaviour.'

'You deserve to fail, and you *will*!' Carmelo wrenched himself free, as Elliott finally released his grip. 'I do much better elsewhere.'

'Good luck with that.' Elliott couldn't see the expression on his former chef's face, as he turned away and marched out of the market, but he'd bet he was looking far less sure of himself than when he'd walked in.

'Well, that certainly made the market more exciting than I was expecting.' Anna laughed, and some of the tension left his shoulders. Whatever problems it caused, he was well shot of Carmelo.

'I'm sorry. I didn't mean for you to get caught in the middle of that, but he had it coming. He can't keep treating people as if they're just there for his entertainment, or as verbal punchbags when things aren't going his way.'

'Don't worry. Like I said, I'm not as fragile as you seem to think I am, and I've dealt with my fair share of temperamental staff over the years. For what it's worth, I think you did the right thing.'

'I don't suppose you know any decent chefs who might be on the lookout for a job?' Even if he could persuade Sara to come back and take on the role of head chef, he'd still need to find her a sous chef, and fast.

'I don't know, I could ask around.' She looked at him thoughtfully for a moment. 'But if you're really desperate, I could fill in for a week or two, just until you can get some more cover.'

'You'd do that, really?'

'Uh-huh, but maybe don't ask me again, in case I realise how crazy it is and change my mind.' She wrinkled her nose. 'I just figured, as you saved me and Albie last night, it's the least I could do.'

'That would be amazing. Thank you so much. This is a real imposition, but do you think you might be able to start today? I'll try ringing Sara in a minute, but we're fully booked this week, so I'm going to need you both.'

'I'll have to bring Albie.'

'Of course, and if there's anything else you need, just say the word.'

'Maybe just my head read.' She laughed again.

'You won't regret it, I promise.' Working at the adventure centre could be the perfect distraction for Anna, he just had to keep reminding himself that she was in Port Kara to mend a broken heart. Whatever connection he felt to her was his problem, and he was determined to keep it that way.

3

By the time Anna got back to pick up Albie from where Greg and the others were still drinking coffee on the harbour-side, she was already regretting the offer she'd made to Elliott. She'd rented Myrtle Cottage for a stress-free summer, and now she was going to spend at least the next couple of weeks in a sweltering kitchen, cooking for city types who had more money than sense. They must do, if they wanted to spend their spare time hanging off the side of cliffs, or potholing in the network of narrow tunnels that even some of the smugglers had chosen to avoid.

Elliott had been on the phone the whole time they'd been walking back to pick up Albie. First, to the centre, to warn them that Carmelo was on the way and that they needed to keep an eye on him; then to Sara, desperately trying to talk her into coming back to work now that her ex was out of the picture.

As soon as they collected Albie, they were going straight to the centre and Anna would be cooking lunch for thirty people, with or without Sara's help. That bit didn't worry her; it was the thought of being back in a restaurant kitchen, surrounded by other people with their own emotions and problems, which made it feel as though her heart was beating in her head. When Finn died, she'd attempted to bury herself in work, thinking it would help. But when one of the team members had lost his temper about a missed order of oyster mushrooms, she'd had the mother of all meltdowns, in front of half the staff and within earshot of the packed restaurant. She'd thrown a frying pan against the wall, narrowly missing taking out one of the commis chefs with it. The fury had taken her breath away. How could anyone think having the wrong type of mushroom mattered when Finn was gone? Didn't they realise that *nothing* mattered anymore?

She'd walked out the moment the frying pan had clattered onto the tiled floor and she hadn't stopped until she'd reached the heath; collapsing into a sobbing heap, which made even the friendliest dog walkers keep a wide berth. That was when she'd realised she couldn't do it anymore. She couldn't deal with other people's petty problems when her heart had been ripped in two. Within days, the restaurant was on the market, and she'd stayed in the background until a buyer was finally found. Dealing with the finances and marketing was something she could manage. It was just people she struggled with, when the only person she really wanted was gone for good.

'Thank goodness for that.' Elliott let go of a long breath. 'Sara has agreed to come back, but she's eighty miles away at her mum's place already, so she's not going to make it back in time for the lunch service. We've got a packed schedule of activities this afternoon, so we'll need to have everyone fed by two at the latest. We usually start serving at half past twelve, but I've asked the bar manager to put up a notice to say we won't be serving lunch until one today.'

'What are you like at chopping veg and taking instructions?' Anna tilted her head. If he wanted a solution to the mess he was in, then he was going to have to get his hands dirty.

'I'm probably better at the first thing than the second. But, right now, I'm more than willing to accept the advice of an expert.'

'It'll be more like orders than advice; we're going to be up against it.' Anna ran her hand over Albie's soft head. It had been her go-to form of stress relief for months, and she was going to need him more than ever now. 'How many other staff have you got in the kitchen?'

'There are three commis chefs, who work on a part-time rota basis. Then there are a couple of casual staff who come in to do the washing up and things like that, when we're busy. With Sara and Carmelo gone, there's just one of the young commis chefs, Billy, in the kitchen at the moment. He was almost hyperventilating when I spoke to him, especially when I told him Carmelo was on the way back to pick up his stuff.'

'Poor kid.' Anna ran a hand through her hair. 'Well if it's just me and Billy, I'm definitely going to need your help.'

'No problem. I'll get one of the other guides to get everything ready for my activities this afternoon.'

'What have you got planned?' Anna looked across at Greg, who was already rounding up the rest of the diving party and heading back to the minibus, emblazoned with the Dorton Adventure Centre logo. It was parked to the left of a row of beach huts, about fifty feet from where they were standing.

'We're coasteering.' Elliott smiled at the look of confusion that no doubt crossed her face. 'Sorry, the terminology has become like second nature to me. Coasteering is exploring the coast-line using a combination of climbing and swimming. We take the clients up through some of the old smugglers' caves and then they get another adrenaline fix by swimming through some of the rapids and whirlpools that the cliff formations create. For those who want to, we finish it off with some cliff jumps into the sea, but not everyone wants to go through with that.'

'I can see why.' Anna shivered. When Albie had been scrabbling on the edge of the cliff, the whole sea below him had looked like one big whirlpool. Why anyone would want to jump from a cliff out of choice, she'd never know. But Finn would have loved it, and he would almost certainly have got on with Elliott too.

'It's far less scary than the thought of facing thirty guests with very high expectations, wanting their lunch.'

'You stick to what you do best and I'll stick to what I do best. How's that for a deal?' If Elliott tried to coerce her into joining in with his activities that would definitely be a deal breaker, but he was nodding his head.

'Absolutely.' He gestured towards the Land Rover parked behind the minibus, which was also emblazoned with the Dorton Adventure Centre logo. 'Shall we put Albie in my car and head up? The clock's ticking.'

'I guess we better had then, unless you think we can pass off some slices of cheese piled next to a piece of toast as the latest deconstructed must-eat dish?'

'Nothing wrong with cheese on toast, but at the prices we're charging, I think they might expect a bit more.'

'We'd better make sure we give them their money's worth, then.'

Following him to the car, Anna was already running through recipes in her head. Elliott had told her they'd had some Cornish cod delivered earlier. So, as long as Carmelo hadn't slung it in the nearest dumpster, it should be pretty easy to pull something together that would meet the guests' expectations.

Elliott turned and smiled as he reached the car, and an uncomfortable feeling settled in Anna's stomach. She was just doing this to repay the debt she owed him, that was all. In a couple of weeks, it would just be her and Albie hanging out together back at the cottage — what could possibly go wrong?

★   ★   ★

'You're not as bad at this as you said you'd be.' Anna looked across from plating up the last portion of baked Cornish cod in caramelised honey, as Elliott chopped up strawberries to accompany the dark chocolate Chantilly she'd made for dessert. Having tasted both dishes, he could say, hand on heart, that they were far better than anything Carmelo had made.

'It must have been all those years in the boy scouts, getting our dinner ready for the campfire.' It was just as well he was on chopping duty and had to keep

69

his eyes on what he was doing, otherwise he'd have been looking at Anna every time she looked across at him. For the first time, he understood what Carmelo had meant when he'd described himself as an artist. Watching her turn simple ingredients into some of the most delicious dishes he'd ever tasted, as well as whipping up a spaghetti Pomodoro for the guests who didn't like fish, was nothing short of miraculous. She was so calm; there was none of the drama there'd been with Carmelo, and she was really patient with Billy, too, even though he'd stuttered like a schoolboy for the first forty-five minutes.

'You'd better get a move on with that veg,' Anna grinned, 'because there's a big pile of washing up, and Billy can't do all of that as well.'

Carmelo had done what damage he could when he'd turned up to collect his stuff. Billy had guarded the kitchen, with the help of Jonathan, the new bar manager, to stop him sabotaging any of the stock. But he'd still managed to phone the casual staff who usually did the washing up and tell them that they were being replaced by kids on work experience, because the centre was too tight to pay a proper wage.

When Elliott had rung them to see if they could come in and help out with lunch, now that they were down a staff member, one of them had been out and the other one had burst into tears. It had taken him ten minutes to calm her down and get the full story, but he'd managed to sort it out in the end. Trouble was, she was so upset by what Carmelo had said that she was in no fit state to come into work. Anna had just shrugged and said they'd manage somehow, and he liked her all the more because of it.

'Billy's been brilliant, don't you think?' Elliott stopped chopping again, as Anna took the first tray of desserts out of the fridge.

'He's great. He really listens, and I can see the passion in his eyes when

71

he's working with the food. I think he's got the potential to be very good, with the right training. Where did you find him?'

'All the commis chefs are studying catering part-time and working here the rest of the time, but I think you're right: Billy has got the most potential.' Elliott had sent Billy out to the bar to get himself an iced drink. He'd worked non-stop, doing everything Anna asked him to, and getting through as much of the clearing up in between as he possibly could. He deserved a quick break, and, for a few minutes, Elliott and Anna had the kitchen to themselves. 'Have you trained chefs before?'

'I don't mind you asking me questions, as long as you keep chopping!' Anna was like a different person when she laughed. 'But, yes, I've been involved with training a few chefs and I can already see that Billy's got what it takes.'

'This catering business of yours obviously wasn't a burrito stall or

72

burger van on the side of the motorway, was it?'

'Not exactly, although I had one of the best meals of my life from a burrito stall at a street market in California.' Anna had an uncanny knack of changing the subject, when he got too close to finding out more about her. 'Do you think Albie's okay?'

'Jonathan got one of the bar staff to take him for a walk earlier, but I'm sure he's been making himself at home on my sofas.' They'd put the dog in Elliott's apartment when they'd first got back to the centre, and he'd heaved himself straight up onto one of the sofas in front of the floor-to-ceiling windows that looked out on the sea, barking at the seagull sitting brazenly on the balcony outside.

'I like the fact that you didn't shout at him to get off straight away. Anyone who's nice to Albie automatically goes up in my estimation.'

'Why don't you go and check up on him when Billy gets back? I think we can cope with garnishing the Chantilly.'

'Are you sure?'

'Absolutely. You've more than earned half an hour off. Let me just do the first one before you go, and you can let me know if I've got it right.' Elliott fanned some slices of strawberry on to the plate, next to the pot of Chantilly, and drizzled some strawberry jus and cream next to it.

'You just need to swirl the jus a bit more artistically.' Anna put her hand over his, moving it so that it made a far nicer pattern as he squeezed the bottle. His body reacted to her touch and he pulled his hand away.

'I think I've got it from here.' He turned away from her as the young commis chef came back into the kitchen. 'But I'm sure Billy can give me a bit of advice if I need it. Go and check on Albie and see if he's got rid of that seagull. I'll pop up before I take my clients out coasteering.'

'I'll see you later then.' Anna stopped and gave Billy a quick hug. 'And well done you, you've been an absolute superstar.'

'Anna's amazing, isn't she?' Billy said, as Anna walked out of the kitchen. He had gone bright red again, but this time it had nothing to do with the heat.

'Yeah, she's great.' Elliott tried to concentrate on plating up the Chantilly. It wasn't going to be easy having Anna around, and keeping the distance she obviously wanted. But she was going to be good for the business, and that was his number one priority. Everything else was just fleeting.

★   ★   ★

'How did the Chantilly go down?' Anna had her hand resting on Albie's head when Elliott walked back into the apartment. It was weird being in a virtual stranger's flat, sitting on his sofa with her dog as if she owned the place.

'There were lots of compliments for the chef.' Elliott sat down on the other side of Albie. 'Do you think you could

75

bear to do it again tonight, and stick around until I can get someone else in?'

'I enjoyed it, actually. Maybe getting back to work somewhere different was what I needed.' She could have laid down on the sofa and fallen asleep, given half a chance, but at least the exhaustion stopped her mind whirring for a while.

'I'll pay you, of course. Carmelo was on fifty pounds an hour, if that sounds fair? I know it's not London rates.'

'I don't need you to pay me, but you can donate whatever you think is fair to the lifeboat station.' Anna ran her hand over Albie's soft head again. 'I'd rather they benefitted. Someone in a situation like Finn's might need them one day. And if I can help them be there when they're needed, even a little bit, then I'll happily stay on for as long as you need someone.'

'Whatever you want me to do with the money is fine by me, but I volunteer with the lifeboat crew, so I know how grateful they are of all the donations they can get.' Elliott rubbed Albie's ear and the dog thumped his tail against the sofa. The seagull that had been taunting him all afternoon reappeared on the balcony, strutting like Mick Jagger crossing a stage. Suddenly it pecked at the glass, and Albie shot off the sofa and ran straight into the window pane, hitting it with a thud.

'Are you okay, buddy?' Elliott was on his feet before Anna and he rubbed the dog's head gently. 'I don't think he's done himself any harm, but maybe I should pull the blind down so the seagull doesn't keep taunting him.'

'Thank you.' Anna patted her leg and the dog trotted over to her. 'And I don't just mean for looking after Albie.'

'I'm the one who should be thanking you, after everything you've done today.'

'Let's just agree to be thankful that Albie's antics brought us together on that coastal path, shall we?' Anna patted the dog again. 'Someone obviously realised we could help each other out.'

She'd been about to say that someone had realised they needed each other, but that sounded too personal. It was like pulling the blind down on Albie's tormentor — some things were best kept firmly behind a barrier.

4

Anna's first two weeks working at the adventure centre had passed in a blur. She was splitting most of the cooking duties with Sara, so she'd been able to have a lie-in on Sunday morning, before heading up to the centre in time to help out with Sunday lunch — when both she and Sara would be working together. Usually, they took turns to cook breakfast, then one of them led the lunch service and one of them the evening, with the commis chefs splitting the shifts between them. There'd been a few occasions when they'd needed to work together, though. There were the gala dinners on Friday nights and the farewell lunches on Sundays just before the guests checked out, before a brief hiatus until the next group of guests checked in on Monday morning. It meant the centre was always empty on

Sunday evenings, and Anna suspected it was the only time Elliott took off.

Walking up to the centre with Albie in tow, she'd spotted Elliott coming back with a group of guests in one of the minibuses, the roof stacked high with surfboards. Finn was never far from her thoughts, and just catching a glimpse of a surfboard could hit her like a physical blow to the stomach. But, when she was working, whole chunks of time passed when he wasn't at the forefront of her mind. She'd even woken, on the morning of the last gala dinner, thinking about what she needed to prepare for that, rather than Finn being constantly on her mind from the moment she opened her eyes. It wasn't until she got up and let Albie out, spotting a surfer already riding the waves in the distance, that it hit her all over again.

'Sorry, darling.' She'd said the words out loud and Albie had turned to look at her, thinking she was talking to him, as she so often did these days. Finn might not be able to hear her, but she'd wanted to apologise anyway. How could she be pushing his loss further down the list? Grabbing her mobile phone, she scrolled through the photos from their last trip to Cornwall, trying to remember the feel of his arms around her. She couldn't let her memory of him start to fade; it was all she had left.

'What's for lunch today, then?' Elliott called out and raised his hand, bringing her back to the present.

'The main course is up to Sara. I'm just the assistant chef today.' Anna gestured towards the dog, who was already pulling on his lead. 'I'm just going to put Albie up in the apartment, if that's okay? I think he's keen to get settled in his favourite sunny spot.'

'No problem. I've made sure all my good shoes are safely locked away!' Elliott grinned and Albie wagged his tail in response, as if he knew he was the topic of conversation. In the first week Anna had worked at the centre, Albie had done something he hadn't

81

done since he was a puppy, and eaten one of Elliott's Gucci loafers. He didn't miss a beat, though, dismissing the seven-hundred-pound pair of shoes as ridiculously impractical for his life down in Cornwall. Instead, he'd gone out and spent nearly as much on toys and other bits for Albie, including a slow-release ball filled with treats, and a doggy sofa that was probably more comfortable than the lumpy one the rental company had put in Myrtle Cottage. No wonder Albie was trying to drag her towards Elliott; he was the dog's new favourite person.

★　★　★

'I still think you should be serving cream with that. Seems pointless to make home-made sorbet, when I bet nearly everyone would rather have cream to take off the tartness of the pie.' Sara was standing so close to Anna that, if she'd taken a step backwards, she could have stood on her toes. And there were times, during the course of preparing the Sunday lunch together, that Anna had been sorely tempted.

'The sorbet is quite sweet and I've always found it has a lightness that can lift the tart. But if anyone wants cream instead, I'll make sure the servers know to say it's available.'

Anna had prepared most of the desserts the day before, including the sorbet, which had been frozen overnight, so she just had the plating-up to supervise. She'd been assistant chef to Sara during the main course and had literally bitten her lip a few times to stop herself commenting on the way Sara spoke to Billy, the young commis chef. She'd been tempted to suggest some ideas for preparing the main course with a bit more imagination, too, but since she was leaving as soon as Elliott found a replacement, there was no point risking upsetting Sara and leaving him with the task of finding two new chefs, instead of one.

'Carmelo would never have done it

that way.' Sara sniffed. 'But he had a magician's touch when it came to combining flavours, so I suppose you can't expect to live up to that.'

'I wouldn't try.' Anna forced a brightness into her voice that she didn't feel. 'I know you miss Carmelo, but I won't be here for much longer and, with any luck, Elliott will manage to find a new chef who has a similar magic touch.'

'It won't be the same.' Sara sighed and Anna caught Billy's eye. She'd immediately warmed to the young trainee chef, who seemed to love the buzz of working at the centre and always had the latest gossip on which celebrities had been spotted in Port Kara.

'I don't know why you keep harping on about Carmelo; he treated you worse than a dog most of the time.' Billy had a lilting Cornish accent that Anna could have listened to all day, as well as enough courage to stand up to Sara by giving it to her straight.

'You wouldn't understand, *William*.' Sara's tone was sharp in comparison and she emphasised Billy's full name. 'I had a connection with Carmelo that went beyond what most people can comprehend. If waitresses like Darcy throw themselves at him, then that's hardly his fault, is it? He's got an aura.'

Elliott strode into the kitchen just in time to catch what Sara had said, and, as Anna smiled in his direction, she had to fight to stop herself from laughing. It was difficult to believe Sara wasn't joking, especially as Elliott had been made to promise that there was no chance of Carmelo being reinstated before she'd agreed to return. In less than two weeks she seemed to have had a complete change of heart about her ex.

'The trouble with Carmelo was that he was willing to share his aura with almost anyone.' Elliott's response was deadpan, and Anna concentrated on slicing up one of the pecan pies she'd made to go with the hazelnut cream, so that she didn't catch his eye again. She wouldn't be able to hold it in, if she did. She placed the first row of desserts on the kitchen line where the servers picked up the food; they were whipped away by the waiting staff almost as soon as she'd set them down. It was time for a change of subject.

'Come on then, Billy; you must have heard some more about who's bought the beach house at Figgy Bay?' Anna looked over at him as she spoke. The beach house had apparently been on the market for a cool three million, and everyone at the centre had been talking for days about who might have bought it.

'I certainly have, but I was a bit gutted to discover it wasn't a young, good looking millionairess with a trust fund, whose only desire is to find a penniless commis chef to settle down with.' Billy grinned at Anna.

'Girls like that aren't the ones you want, Billy, trust me.' Elliott looked from Billy to Anna, and back again. 'They're usually more in love with the money than they are with anyone, or anything, else. You want to find yourself a girl with interests similar to yours.

They might say opposites attract, but it rarely works in the long term if you're too different.'

'Are you going to come out with it, or just stand there wasting more time when you should be getting on with your job. I know you're just a trainee, but some of us take it seriously.' Sara snapped at Billy, who just smiled in response. She was clearly still smarting from the comments he'd made about her and Carmelo.

'Now, now, don't you be getting like that with me because you can't stand the suspense. I'm just building up the excitement, that's all.' Billy grinned again. 'I still remember when I was a little kid and the biggest news in Port Kara was the lifeboat house getting a fresh coat of paint. It's only in the last few years that the rich and famous have started to flock here. So I'm making the most of it, while it lasts!'

'It's locals like you that make Port Kara the place it is, though, and that's why so many people want to come here.' Elliott said, earning Billy a filthy look from Sara.

'I agree and, whoever it is, they'd be lucky to live in the same town as you.' Anna smiled and she meant every word, even if a tiny part of her was enjoying Sara's reaction to Billy being the centre of attention for once.

'See, these two know how to get me to spill my secrets.' Billy waved the tea towel he was holding with a flourish that a magician would have been proud of. 'The rumour is that Jasper Holland's put in an offer on the house.'

'Really?' Sara looked the most animated Anna had seen her all week. 'Who'd have thought we'd have an Oscar winner in our midst . . . I know he's nearly sixty but I still wouldn't kick him out of bed! I read somewhere that he's a bit of an adrenaline junkie too.'

'I saw an article about that as well!' Billy was really fired up now. 'He could become one of our regulars.' Most of the guests were residents on week-long stays, but non-residents could also book events on a daily or half-day basis. The other staff had told Anna that the centre had already catered for a number of celebrities who owned holiday homes in Port Kara.

'If we can get him involved in the centre then I'd be more than happy to have him as a new neighbour.' Elliott frowned as he met Anna's gaze, and she just hoped he couldn't read her expression. Jasper Holland definitely wasn't someone she wanted as a neighbour, no matter how good it might be for the centre.

'You don't look very excited, Anna. Don't you know who *Jasper Holland* is?' Sara said his name in the slow, over-exaggerated way that someone might use to give a non-English speaker instructions.

'I've heard of him.' She shrugged, almost as eager to change the subject as when Sara was talking about Carmelo. 'Billy, can you put these plates on the line, please?'

'Yes, Chef.' Billy's response earned him another daggered look from Sara, and Anna carried on plating up the desserts as Billy moved them to the line. Sara was still talking about Jasper Holland, but Anna couldn't bring herself to pretend she was excited about his imminent arrival. If she'd told the others that she'd known Jasper for years, they probably wouldn't have believed her. Even if they had, it would have led to non-stop questions, and he was a part of her life she wanted to forget — the friend who'd first encouraged Finn to start surfing, and a reminder of their old life together. The actor may just have won his third Oscar, but if Finn had never met Jasper Holland, he might still be around, and Anna had no desire to see someone who would rake up all those feelings.

'Can I borrow you for a minute, Anna?' Elliott's voice behind her almost made her jump. She'd been miles away, years away too; with Finn back at the forefront of her mind, where he belonged, she'd almost forgotten Elliott was there. The sensation of his breath on the back of her neck made her skin tingle, though, and the heady scent of his aftershave was something she only associated with Elliott. Try as she might to pretend he hadn't stirred something in her — something she'd assumed was gone for ever — her body betrayed her all too often.

'Of course, I'm sure Billy can manage to plate up the last few desserts.' Elliott's hand accidentally brushed against hers, and she could almost sense Sara watching them. Sara had made a play for Elliott in the first week after Carmelo had been sacked, but it had been clear to everyone that he wasn't interested, and Anna had felt sorry for the new head chef. Maybe that's why Sara's feelings about Carmelo had come back with such a vengeance — she obviously wanted someone in her life, and it clearly wasn't going to be Elliott. 'Is there a problem?'

'The opposite, actually.' Elliott smiled. 'There are some diners who want to give their compliments to the chef, for the dessert.'

'Oh no, really?' Heat rose up Anna's neck and, if looks could kill, she'd be lying on the kitchen floor with Sara standing over her body, and the contents of the knife block sticking out of her back.

'Yes and they're insistent they want to speak to you. Apparently the lemon tart and sorbet is . . . ' He paused for a moment. 'I think the word they used was *exquisite.*'

'I'd rather not.' Anna pulled a face. 'It's a team effort, anyway.'

'It's just for a minute, I promise. One of them is the CEO of a bank who could put an awful lot of business our way, if he leaves here with as big a smile on his face as he had when he finished up his dessert.' Elliott held her gaze and for a moment she couldn't move; she wanted to say no, but for some reason the words wouldn't come.

'If you think it will make that big a difference, then I'll do it. But it really should be Sara going out there — she's the head chef.' Anna turned towards

92

Sara, who had an expression that wouldn't have looked out of place on a fishmonger's counter. But before she could change her mind, Elliott caught hold of her hand and more or less dragged her out of the kitchen and through to the dining room.

'Hugo, this is Anna. She's the one responsible for that dessert you've been raving about.' Elliott stopped by a table of eight guests, directing his comment at a dark-haired man sitting at the head of the table.

'The lemon tart was amazing. Elliott made sure I got to try some of the pecan pie too and let me tell you something: I've eaten at top restaurants all over the world and had some weird and wonderful creations — even something called raspberry air — but your desserts are something else. If you're ever on the lookout for another job, I'd be willing to make you a very good offer as executive chef at the bank's head-quarters.'

'Hey, Hugo, you didn't tell me you'd

try and poach my staff if I brought Anna out here!' Elliott's tone was jokey, but his smile didn't reach his eyes in the way it usually did.

'I didn't get where I am today by being shy about going after what I want.' Hugo put an arm around the gorgeous blonde woman sitting next to him and laughed. 'How else do you think I persuaded someone like Caro to marry me?'

'It's a really great offer, but I'm not looking for anything else right now.' Anna took the card that Hugo slid across the table anyway, and put it in her pocket. 'But it's lovely to hear you enjoyed the desserts so much. Although it's really a team effort; there's a young commis chef out in the kitchen who you might want to make that job offer to in a year or so.'

'If Elliott's got any sense, he won't let either of you go.'

'I'm not intending to, if I can help it.' Elliott caught her eye again and gave her an apologetic smile. She hoped it was all just for Hugo's benefit — she'd been straight with Elliott from the start. This was just a temporary arrangement.

Suddenly their conversation was interrupted by a loud bang as someone threw the kitchen doors open with considerable force. Anna turned her head just as Sara charged in.

'So this is how it's going to be, is it? Because the two of you are sleeping together, she's going to get all the praise? You bring her out here when someone wants to give their compliments to the chef, and I'm left in the kitchen supervising Forrest Gump.' Sara had crossed the room in a few steps, the veins in her neck visibly protruding.

'There's nothing going on between me and Elliott.' Heat flushed across Anna's cheeks, which made it look all the more like she was lying.

'Don't take me for an idiot. I've seen the way you two look at each other, it's obvious even to that ape Billy that the two of you are at it like rabbits.'

'Sara, that's enough. If you've got a

problem, I suggest we talk about it in the kitchen.' Elliott's voice was eerily calm, but there was a muscle going in his cheek, and everyone on Hugo's table was staring blatantly in their direction. Thankfully, most of the other diners had already left, except for another table of guests on the far side of the restaurant, who were just being served their desserts by one of the waiters.

Sara looked at him for a moment, weighing up her options, then turned on her heel and stalked back into the kitchen, with Elliott close behind her.

'I'm sorry about that.' Anna turned to Hugo, who was watching her with a smile on his face.

'It's not a problem. I like Elliott's style. There's only one way to deal with employees like that — firmly — and I think your boss has got a handle on it.' Hugo laughed.

'I hope it hasn't spoilt your stay.' Anna paused. Elliott probably wouldn't thank her for saying what she was about to say, but she did it anyway. 'I know he's hoping your bank might want to make more use of the centre in the future.'

'Even if the only thing on offer here was a repeat of your lemon tart, I'd definitely be recommending it to the Board. But this has been a great trial run for our senior management's team-building events, and we've all been really impressed with Elliott, haven't we?' Hugo turned to his beautiful young wife, who nodded in response. 'Seeing the way he can handle himself in this side of the business, when he literally had our lives in his hands yesterday as we were abseiling down those cliffs, only convinces me more that this is the right place for us.'

'You won't regret it.' Anna nodded. Now wasn't the time to tell him that nothing she made would be on the menu next time he came back. If people were picking up on how she felt about Elliott, then it was only a matter of time before he did too and that was the last thing she wanted. She had to get out while she still could and, as soon as he'd sorted things out with Sara, she'd tell him she was leaving.

★   ★   ★

'I've never been good enough for you, have I? Not as head chef or anything else. Not since Little Miss Perfect came along with the sob story about her dead husband. It's probably all a lie to get you to feel sorry for her, but it seems to work. Did you start off by comforting her and then one thing led to another?' Sara's eyes were open so wide that white was visible all the way around the iris, and she barely seemed to notice when Anna walked back into the kitchen.

'Get out!' Elliott's face was like a mask, and Anna wanted the ground to open up and swallow her. She'd told the others as little as she could get away with about her past, but she'd admitted to being widowed. Having it discussed like this hadn't been part of the bargain, though. She'd agreed to help out if Elliott let her remain anonymous, hidden away in the kitchen, too busy for a few hours each day to think about Finn, or anything else for that matter. Now Sara was laying her grief raw, for everyone to pick over, and if she looked up, she was certain she'd see *that* look in their eyes — the sympathy she hated so much, because it reminded her all over again just how much she'd lost.

'You can't just order me out; I'm entitled to have my say and I'm sick to death of the way you're treating her like she's some sort of Messiah who saved the restaurant after Carmelo left.'

'I can do whatever I like, including ordering you out, seeing as you're in *my* kitchen. You might not like the way you're being treated, but that's open to interpretation. What isn't, is the way you've treated the other kitchen staff, including Anna, and the embarrassment you've caused our guests. That's not how things work here, Sara. We've all made allowances for you after what happened with Carmelo, but there's no excuse for the way you've acted today.' Elliott spoke through clenched teeth and the realisation of what he was saying finally seemed to be dawning on her.

'You're sacking me?'

'If that's how you want to put it, or you could say I'm letting you go. Whatever makes it easier for you to get another job — anything you want, as long as it gets you out of here faster.' Elliott moved to the kitchen door and held it open.

'Carmelo was right, you are an idiot, but you've made it easier for me. He's asked me to go and join him in the restaurant he's working at now, so we can make a fresh start. He said all along that bringing Anna in was your plan, ever since you started sleeping with her. I didn't know whether to trust him or not, but it's obvious now that everything he's said is true and I should never have believed you, or the lies that waitress spread about Carmelo in the first place.'

'There's nothing going on between — '

Anna's words were lost in the sound of Sara slamming the kitchen door behind her.

'I'm sorry about that. I seem to be making a habit of sacking my head chefs of late.' Elliott barely had time to get the words out before Billy started to cheer.

'If it hadn't been her leaving, it would have been me.' Billy shrugged, when he eventually stopped cheering. One of the waitresses, who'd been in the kitchen at the time, nodded in agreement.

'Me too, and most of the other waiting staff said the same. We've all said this week that we've had enough. Carmelo was bad, but she's even worse.'

'And what about you?' Elliott turned to Anna and she gave a small nod of her head.

'I was going to tell you later that I wasn't coming back after tonight.' She couldn't bring herself to look at him, in case her face gave away the real reason she'd felt she needed to get out. Blaming Sara was a welcome excuse.

'But now Sara's gone, please tell me you're willing to stay on?' Elliott's tone was urgent, and part of her wanted to bolt out of the door behind Sara. He *needed* her, but she was starting to realise she *wanted* him, and that made her the worst person in the world — she was betraying Finn every time she looked at Elliott. Sara had seen it and everyone else probably did too. She could imagine what they were all thinking: *poor widowed Anna, and now she's got a crush on Elliott.* She should be taking the opportunity to run while she could, and hide out at Myrtle Cottage for the rest of the summer. But when she finally looked up at Elliott, she knew she couldn't do it.

'I can hardly leave you in the lurch, the way you're getting through chefs, can I?' She tried to laugh, but it didn't quite come out right.

'Don't worry. Billy and the other commis chefs are off from college for the summer, so they can all do more hours, and we can get some agency staff in. I can help out in the kitchen if you need me to, like I did when Carmelo first left, at least until we find someone new.' Elliott's offer was meant to be reassuring, but it just layered on the guilt. She shouldn't want to work so closely with him, but she did, and picturing Finn couldn't push those thoughts out of her head anymore. Even as she wrestled with her guilt, she was thinking of ways to spend more time with Elliott. It was wrong, but she just wasn't ready to walk away.

* * *

'I needed this; thanks for staying.' Elliott looked across at Anna as he spoke. She was almost entirely in shadow, except for the little bit of light cast on her face by the table lamp on the other side of the lounge. It was dark enough to make out the lights on the boats out in the bay. Albie was lying between their feet, snoring and occasionally flicking his back legs, as if he was running in his dreams.

'I often don't feel like cooking when I get back to Myrtle Cottage, anyway, it's just not the same cooking for one. Sometimes there are definite benefits to working in a restaurant.' After they'd finished clearing up the kitchen, and the others had set off for home, Anna had suggested they share some of the leftovers from the Sunday lunch. It had been a long day, and when she'd offered to come up to the flat to eat with him, before heading home, he hadn't taken much persuading. 'Although I don't know if I should be here, Elliott . . . '

'Why not?'

'Because of what Sara said.' Her voice caught in her throat and she closed her eyes, tipping her head back. 'If everyone at the centre thinks you're showing me some kind of favouritism, maybe we shouldn't add any fuel to the fire.'

'She's just lashing out because she's jealous of your ability. I think she was from the moment she first tasted something you cooked. She couldn't compete and she knew it. I'm convinced that's why she got back in touch with Carmelo and he managed to talk her around.'

'As long as you're sure. I wouldn't want to cause problems with anyone else at the centre.'

'Do you think I treat you differently to the other staff?' He watched her face, as she finally opened her eyes again. He'd tried really hard to keep his attraction to Anna in check, but maybe he hadn't been as good at that as he'd thought he was. It wasn't just because she was beautiful, either; she really was brilliant at what she did, and Sara had every reason to be jealous. But she also had this air of fragility, just below the veneer of toughness she managed to maintain by throwing herself into work, and he didn't want to be the one to fracture that.

'I don't know, maybe you do, but then I'm in a different position to everyone else, aren't I? I'm volunteering for a charitable donation to the lifeboat station, and we both know that I'll be going soon. That must change the dynamic between us, and Sara can't be the only one to see it.'

'I suppose so.' Every time she reminded him that she'd be leaving soon, it was like a physical blow. He'd accepted that there couldn't be anything between them, but he was still going to miss her.

'I just think we need to be careful not to give anyone the impression that we're more than colleagues.'

'I thought we were friends?' He wanted that at least. That way, they'd stay in touch and she might even come back to Port Kara again. The prospect of her leaving forever at the end of the summer was pretty depressing.

'We are friends, but all of this, having dinner together — it's not like we invited Billy and the others, is it?' She sighed. 'I know it was my idea, but maybe I need to think these things through a bit more. Just because the two of us are crystal clear that we're only friends, it doesn't mean everyone else will see it that way.'

'I doubt the others have a shred of Sara's bitterness or suspicious nature, so I really don't think you need to worry, and I'm really glad you wanted to have dinner with me. I'd have been up here, otherwise, going over how I should have got rid of Sara when she first started sniping at everyone. I just didn't think we could afford to lose her *and* Carmelo. I'm going to get a reputation at this rate and no-one will ever want to work for the centre.'

'None of this is your fault.' Anna swirled the wine around her glass. Her cheeks had a soft glow in the lamplight, probably helped by the fact that they'd finished a bottle of wine between them. His hands itched to reach out and touch her, and he tried not to imagine what it would be like if she tucked her feet up under her on the sofa and leant against him. Whatever Anna's worries about what other people were thinking, nothing would ever happen between them. But that didn't mean he hadn't thought about it. A lot.

He couldn't picture a casual fling though, as much as that might have got Anna out of his system. The sort of intimacy he pictured in his mind, when he looked at her, was what made her different. It was one of the reasons he hadn't made a move, despite the fact that he thought about her far more often than he should. Anna was the sort of person who made him want a relationship, and he didn't have time for that, any more than he had time to sort out the mess that Sara's departure had left behind — just when the restaurant had been getting back on an even keel. Anna was right, they needed to be careful not to overstep the line between friendship and something else. Getting her advice on the business was sticking to much safer ground.

'Did you have these sorts of issues where you were running your business?'

'Finn did most of the hiring and firing, but every kitchen I've ever worked in has had high staff turnover. It's a stressful environment and a lot of chefs are temperamental with big egos. Unfortunately, you just seem to have picked two of that sort in a row.' She laughed and he couldn't help wondering how different she'd been before she'd lost her husband. Every time she smiled it was like a light going on, but there were other times when he caught himself watching her, and she seemed to be lost in thought, the corners of her mouth down-turned and the sadness in her eyes blatantly obvious. It was so tempting to try and take it away. But even if she responded, when it ended it would just hurt her more. And it *would* end, it had to; their lives were worlds apart. He liked her too much to risk a relationship with her, anyway. His family were no good at relationships, and someone like Anna deserved better than he'd ever be able to give. She'd been through enough.

'And what about you, are you really sure you're okay to stay on a bit longer, until I can get someone to take Carmelo's job and decide what to do about replacing Sara?' Elliott paused for a moment. 'I know you said earlier that you'd stay on for a bit, but I don't want you to feel like you have to.'

'Like I said, I'll stay until you've found a replacement for Carmelo, and I can help out until you replace Sara as well. As long as you really are looking and you promise to double up the efforts now that you've lost a second chef?' She turned her head and he smiled, relief flooding through his veins, and not just because he wasn't going to be left without a head chef.

'The trouble is, you've set me an almost impossible task now. It was relatively easy when I was just looking for a replacement for Carmelo, but now I need to find someone to match up to you . . . ' He reached out and touched her arm briefly, feeling her tense in response so that he dropped his hand back down. 'I need to thank you for something else, too, by the way. Hugo left me a message to say he'd enjoyed the entertainment in the restaurant, almost as much as he'd enjoyed the food you'd cooked. He's going to be using the centre for all his management team-building events for the next year, and he'll review it again after that.'

'You see, today hasn't turned out that badly after all. Albie's clearly had a relaxing day.' She looked down at the dog, whose snoring was steadily gaining in volume.

'None of the days since you started here have turned out badly.' He watched her as he spoke. She couldn't seem to look at him, which was probably for the best. If she did, there was a chance he wouldn't be able to stop himself crossing the line, and no good could come of that. At best he might lose her friendship and his third chef in less than a month, and the worst case scenario didn't even bear thinking about. 'Were you tempted by Hugo's job offer? I saw you take his card.'

'I was just doing it to be polite.

Working as a corporate chef doesn't really appeal to me.'

'It would mean heading back to London, too. That's something I don't think I could ever contemplate.' Elliott gestured towards the window. 'Not when it would mean swapping it for a view like this.'

'That's where we differ. Much as I love it here, I can't ever really see myself leaving London permanently. I think it's in my blood. It's where Finn and I met, and where we built our business and our home, and sooner or later it will draw me back in.'

'I hope you change your mind.' Elliott bent down and stroked Albie, who didn't even stir. 'I'll miss you both when you go.' It was as close as he was going to come to telling her how he felt.

'He'll miss you too. But I'd better get the old boy back home to his bed, before he starts thinking he actually lives here.' Anna was already on her feet, and the fact she hadn't mentioned missing Elliott wasn't lost on him. She wasn't ready for anything new, casual or otherwise, at least not with him; even if he'd been willing to take the risk of a summer fling.

'Let me walk you home.'

'No need, he might be a lazy old thing, but Albie can spring into action if I need him.' Anna shook her head to emphasise the point. 'And Port Kara is hardly a crime hotspot. I think we're pretty safe, especially as I can go back the beach way.' Elliott knew that at high tide Myrtle Cottage was cut off to cars, and the only way back was down a set of stone steps cut into the cliff face, which led to a locked tunnel that ended up in the cottage's back garden. It was spooky enough in the daytime, and there was no way he'd even think of letting her go back that way on her own at night. But she suddenly seemed desperate to get out and, at low tide, he couldn't even use the spooky tunnel as an excuse to insist on walking her home.

'Are you sure?'

'We'll be absolutely fine.'

'Can you text me when you get in, to let me know you're safe?' He unlocked the door of the flat, and she finally looked up at him, nodding. 'Thanks again for today.'

'Anytime.' Moving her head, just as he lowered his, her lips brushed against his.

'Oh Anna, I'm sorry. I was just trying to kiss you on the cheek.'

'It's my fault, I moved my head. It was just an accident.' Her words spilled out and she ducked her head again to clip Albie's lead on, seeming glad of the opportunity to move away from him.

'I'll see you tomorrow then?'

'Uh huh.' Fumbling with the door in her haste to get out, she still didn't turn to look at him again, and he had a horrible feeling she wouldn't turn up in the morning. He tried to tell himself that it was the thought of losing a third chef which kept him awake half the night, but Sara had seen it before he'd even admitted it to himself. Despite the reassurances he'd given Anna, he had feelings for her and there was nothing he could do about it, except hope to goodness that they went away.

5

Anna had been doing her best to avoid
spending any time alone with Elliott
since their accidental kiss. He'd been
right that no-one else at the centre
seemed to be making the same
assumption as Sara that there was
something going on between them.
Although that didn't stop the kiss being
on her mind every time she went to
sleep at night, and in the mornings
when she woke up. Their lips had barely
touched but it couldn't have felt more
like a betrayal of Finn, because she
hadn't wanted it to stop. Elliott had
reacted in horror, almost jumping away
from her, but if he'd pulled her into his
arms at the moment she would have
responded. She'd tried to convince
herself that it was just the need for
physical contact, someone other than
Albie to cuddle up to.

There was something about Elliott, though. He wasn't just *anyone* and that's what made it harder. One day she wanted to let someone new into her life. She and Finn had even talked about it, after one of his friends was killed in a motorcycle accident, leaving his young widow behind. Finn had told her that if anything ever happened to him that she should move on and allow herself to find love again. His favourite saying had been 'you only get one life.' It was the reason he used for never being afraid to try something new, and to explain the pure adrenaline thrill he got every time he rode a wave, despite the danger that might lurk beneath. She'd told him to do the same if anything happened to her, but then she'd never been a risk-taker. Unless she'd been in a freak accident with a No.46 bus to Hampstead, she'd be fine. Except she wasn't, she was the one left behind and that was so much harder. Finn had it easy, he didn't have to grieve, or wake up wracked with guilt caused by an almost overwhelming attraction to someone new. Despite what Finn had wanted, it was too soon to get involved in anything serious; that was one thing she did know for certain.

'Come on, Alb. Let's go for another walk.' Albie lifted his head, from where it was resting on his paws, looking less than enthusiastic about the prospect of heading to the beach again. 'I know we've already been once, but it'll do us both good.'

The walls of the cottage felt like they were closing in and it was giving her too much time to think. She could have asked a friend to come down and stay, but she'd wanted the solitude to try and work out where she was going next with her life. The centre was taking up most of her time but when it didn't, the solitude was almost suffocating. She was no nearer to knowing what she wanted to do with this new life, one that didn't have Finn in it, than she had been when she'd arrived. Fifty years or more were stretching in front of her, and the thought was terrifying. Walking on the beach was the only time she felt peaceful, so poor old Albie was getting several long walks a day, whether he wanted them or not.

It was a gloriously sunny Sunday afternoon and the tide was out, so the beach was quite busy. There were some young families making sandcastles and digging in the golden sand, and groups of people who'd clearly come to Port Kara in the hope of doing a bit of celebrity spotting. Why else would you head to the beach wearing Louboutin heels and false eyelashes, like the three girls she passed, who were perched on a picnic blanket taking selfies and giggling?

'I swear, it says on the *Spotted in Port Kara* Instagram feed that Jasper Holland is down here today, and he's supposedly throwing a big party next week. I promise you won't be sorry that we came here instead of going to Ibiza, Alisha. We just need to meet one of his friends and bag ourselves an invite to that party!' One of the girls, who had long red hair cascading in waves over her shoulders, thrust her phone towards her friends, and Anna had to drag Albie away from them before he put big sandy footprints across their blanket.

If the rumours about Jasper were true, then she was going to have to keep a low profile. The last thing she wanted was to bump into the man she held responsible for Finn's death. He'd be happy to entertain the three giggling twenty-somethings who were so eager to hunt him down, though. So she just had to hope that Jasper would be preoccupied, instead of heading down to the surf. If she spotted him clutching a surfboard, like he didn't have a care in the world, she wouldn't be responsible for her actions.

'Hey, I've been calling your name for about two minutes, but you didn't even look up.' Elliott was suddenly standing in front of her, wearing shorts, running shoes, and a t-shirt that clung to his torso. Anna didn't turn around to look at the girls on the blanket again but, if she had, she was certain they'd have been staring in Elliott's direction. The sight of him was enough to make anyone forget all about Oscar winning actors. Trouble was, he also had a knack of making Anna forget about someone far more important.

'Sorry. I was a million miles away. Eavesdropping on a stranger's conversation. It looks like you're making the most of your afternoon off, though.'

'I wanted to have a run before I head down to the lifeboat station for training. I suppose it's not everyone's idea of what to do with an afternoon off, but it works for me.' Elliott reached down and patted Albie's head, as the dog stared up at him with a look of utter devotion.

'How often do you train with the lifeboat crew?'

'At least once a fortnight. We've had a couple of call-outs already this month, but luckily everything turned out okay on both occasions.' Elliott shrugged and Anna bit her lip. He

121

wasn't making this easy: being such a nice guy, looking like he did, and adding life-saving heroics into the mix. She had to remember the promise she'd made herself, though. If she ever did fulfil Finn's wishes and meet someone new, they had to be safe and steady. She definitely didn't want another risk-taker, and Elliott was the opposite of what she was looking for.

'I think it's amazing that all of you volunteer to do that.'

'You're the talk of the lifeboat station, actually.' Elliott grinned. 'In fact, if you and Albie have got time, maybe you could walk down there with me and have a chat to some of the others? They really want to meet you.'

'Do they? Why?'

'Partly because of the money you've been donating, but mostly because of the food you've been sending down. It's made you *very* popular.'

'It's the least I can do.'

'So you'll come down, then?'

'If you really think they'll want me to.

Albie and I need to stretch our legs anyway.' Anna fell into step beside Elliott, as they continued across the sand. The lifeboat station was at the far end of Port Kara beach, on the edge of the horse-shoe shaped harbour that clung to the bottom of the cliff-face on one side.

Billy was working full time in the kitchen as the sous chef during his summer break from college, and Elliott had agreed to try out other chefs from a catering agency, in the hope of finding the right person to take on the head chef's role. They were also using other agency staff to provide cover for days off and holiday leave. The chef who they'd trialled over the last week was okay; but okay wasn't what Elliott wanted for the centre, and Anna had had to agree. It might take a while to find the right person, but at least Elliott was doing something about it now, so he'd seemed to accept that she wouldn't be around for much longer.

'They'll be okay with me bringing Albie into the lifeboat station, won't they? I don't want to risk leaving him tied up outside.' Ever since Anna had started at the centre, she'd been sending desserts down to the crew and it was nice to hear they were appreciated. She kept telling herself it was the only reason she was going to the lifeboat station, it had nothing to do with wanting to be with Elliott.

'Are you kidding, they'll love Albie. He'll probably be their mascot by the time you leave.'

'What have we got coming up at the centre this week?' Anna's hand was only inches away from Elliott's as they walked side-by-side, and her fingers almost involuntarily extended towards his, forcing herself to curl her hand into a tight ball again.

'We've got a big day event booked in for a company called Going Dutch. They want to throw a party at the end of the day, but they want to have it on the beach. So we're going to be pretty busy.'

'Do you usually do that sort of

thing?' Anna couldn't help thinking about the logistics of hosting a party on the beach; all those memories of getting sand in her sandwiches as a child weren't easy to forget.

'If the clients want it, and they're willing to pay enough, then we'll deliver if we can.' Elliott gave her an apologetic smile. 'I know it will give you and Billy a few challenges, but when I set up the adventure centre I wanted to do something different, and to embrace everything the Cornish coast has to offer. What could be better than a beach party, after all?'

'I'll just have to make sure Albie steers clear. It's enough of a nightmare when he gets a whiff of a barbecue when we're on the beach, and he stole a doughnut off a little boy on Tuesday. I had to buy the whole family ice-cream to make it up to them! That's why I'm not letting him off the lead today.'

'You can't blame Albie, it's hard to resist when you see something you really want.' Elliott caught her eye for a moment and the memory of his lips brushing hers caused heat to flood across her cheeks. 'Although sometimes what we want isn't the best thing for us.'

'Hmm. Too many doughnuts aren't good for anyone.' She had no idea if that's what Elliott meant, or if she was reading far too much into it because of how she felt. But she wanted to change the subject either way. 'How long have you been volunteering at the lifeboat station?'

'Ever since I moved down here last year. This is the centre's first full summer season, but it was good to have a release from work whilst I was getting it all set up. It stopped me fixating on the threat of losing everything if the centre failed. Seeing people at their most vulnerable, when their lives could quite literally be swept away, reminded me that even if the worst happened, it wasn't that bad in comparison.'

'I didn't think risks worried you?'

'It's probably the idea that I'd live up

to my father's expectations that worried me the most.'

'Don't you mean *fail* to live up to his expectations?'

'You'd think so.' Elliott didn't look at her as he spoke. 'But he fully expected me to fail; in fact, he told me that I would. He thinks I've thrown everything away by leaving a well-paid job in London to set up what he calls a 'scout-camp for grown-ups'.'

'Has he ever seen what you do?'

'He wouldn't come down here if I paid him. Although he doesn't do much that he isn't paid to do. He's been obsessed with money, and how to make more of it, ever since I can remember. When I was a child, he left the house every morning to head to work in the city, and got home long after I'd gone to bed. I barely knew the man, but I was desperate to make him notice me. That's why I went to work in finance like him, but I felt like I was suffocating from day one.'

'I've got to admit I can't imagine you

in a job like that.' Anna's eyes slid towards him again. Elliott looked like he'd been born to scale the Cornish cliffs, rather than the corporate ladder.

'I can't either, not now. Looking back, I don't know how I did it for so long.'

'Well, the centre's definitely not failing. So your dad can be proud of you.'

'I won't hold my breath. He keeps telling me just how much like my mother I am, and, as far as he's concerned, that's about as insulting as he can get.'

'I take it they aren't together anymore?'

'They always lived separate lives, but when Mum finally realised her dream of opening an art gallery in Brighton, she wasn't around in the tiny pockets of time my father saw fit to make for her.' The bitterness in his voice was obvious. 'That's when he decided that only his personal assistant really understood him. Mum's happier than she's ever been, but she's throwing herself into making her business work and, with the centre to run, I don't get to see her much. As for my father, I haven't seen him since I left my job in London.'

'That's really sad.' It was tempting to tell him that maybe he should offer his father an olive branch. She knew better than anyone that someone could be snatched out of your life permanently without warning, and she was certain Elliott would regret it if that happened before he'd had the chance to make peace with his father. But it was none of her business and she didn't know the whole story. It would be like someone urging her to move on from her life with Finn. She was the only person who'd know when she was ready.

★   ★   ★

'So you're the famous chef we've heard so much about?' Jonty, who headed up the lifeboat crew, shook Anna's hand enthusiastically, and Elliott shot him a look. He'd told his friend not to overplay what he'd said about Anna, but it didn't look like Jonty was going to play ball.

'Hardly famous!' Anna laughed. It was great to see her eyes sparkling like that, and she was like a different person to the one he'd met up on the cliff that first day. She'd saved the centre's reputation by stepping in to help, but he liked to think it had done something for her too. There were still moments when she had that look, which made it obvious that her world had fallen apart, but she was definitely laughing more.

Legend had it that, in the middle ages, there were a group of wise women who lived in Port Kara who specialised in making healing potions. Some locals called them witches, but the guides who worked for the centre all told the same story; people had travelled from all over the country to Port Kara to get their hands on the potions, in an attempt to cure everything from blindness to a broken leg. Maybe some of that magic had rubbed off on Anna, but whatever it was, Port Kara had been good for her. He hoped she'd realise that and decide to stay, but until then he tried not to think about how quickly the weeks were going past. He already found it impossible to imagine going into the kitchen at the centre and not seeing her standing there.

'Put it this way: the crew scramble much more quickly for one of your desserts than they do for a call out.' Jonty hadn't even looked in Elliott's direction since he'd brought Anna into the station, so his warning look had been wasted. 'We've all been wanting to meet you to thank you for donating your wages to the station, as well as for the great food. But Elliott seems keen to keep you to himself.'

'Anna's been busy up at the centre.' All Elliott could do was hope that his tone reminded Jonty what they'd agreed. He'd had to confide in someone how he felt about Anna, and he hadn't wanted to talk to anyone up at the centre. Jonty had told him to go for it, until he'd explained how vulnerable losing her husband had made Anna. But Jonty seemed to have forgotten everything they'd discussed, and Elliott was beginning to regret suggesting that she visit the lifeboat station at all.

'Come on in and I'll introduce you to the others, and bring Albie. We've heard loads about him too.' Jonty still didn't turn and look at Elliott as he led Anna off. Some friend he was.

Grabbing a shower whilst Jonty kept Anna occupied, Elliott tried to focus on the week ahead. He'd gone for a run in the first place to try and get thoughts of her out of his head, but it hadn't been working. Then when he'd spotted her on the beach, he'd wanted a reason to stop her heading in the opposite direction. Visiting the lifeboat station had seemed like a good idea at the time.

'I thought you'd left.' Anna was sitting on one of the seats outside the small galley kitchen which faced the kit room. Albie was lying at her feet, until he saw Elliott and got up; at least one of them was pleased to see him.

'I needed a shower after my run. Did Jonty give you the full tour?'

'He certainly did, and he said you'd replaced these chairs and some of the kitchen equipment with the donations you've made from the centre.' She smiled and the whole room seemed to light up, like it always managed to do somehow.

'The donations are nothing to do with me. It's money you would have earned from your shifts at the centre, if you hadn't decided to donate it.' He smiled, wishing he had another excuse to keep her there. Usually he looked forward to the lifeboat training, but he'd rather have spent the afternoon with Anna. Maybe it was time to get back into the dating game again. Meeting someone else — someone in a position to have the kind of casual relationship he wanted. It might solve the Anna situation. It was a long shot, but nothing else seemed to be working.

'It's a good cause and I don't need the money.' Anna stood up. 'I'd better get on, but I didn't want to leave without saying goodbye. I don't do that anymore . . . just in case.'

'I'm only going training.'

'And Finn was only going surfing.' Anna frowned and he had to clamp his arms to his side to stop himself pulling her towards him.

'I'll be fine and I'll see you in the morning. I promise.'

'Just don't break that promise and let me down, okay?' She gave him such a serious look that he would have done almost anything for her in that moment.

'I won't.' Elliott swallowed hard. He'd keep the promise he made to her and to himself, even if that meant they could never be any more than friends. Something he was finding that idea harder and harder to live with.

★ ★ ★

The lifeboat headed out to sea just as the wind began to pick up, and Anna watched Elliott and the others disappear into the distance.

'Does he remind you of Finn? I can see the resemblance, in a way.' The voice behind Anna was instantly familiar but, when she turned around, she was suddenly unsure.

'Jasper?'

'Guilty as charged, but for heaven's sake keep your voice down. Keeping a low profile is a full-time job.'

'Is the new look for a part?' She raised an eyebrow. The colour of the big bushy beard Jasper was sporting was definitely out of a bottle, and the cap pulled down low over his eyes hid the rest of his face.

'No, it's because this part of Cornwall is full of bearded, surfboarding hipsters and, like this, I blend in. There are far too many autograph-hunters in Port Kara at the moment and I bought the house here to try and get away from all of that.'

'So, it's true then; you bought the beach house at Figgy Bay?'

'I certainly did, but you were the last person I expected to find down here. Until I heard that you were staying at Myrtle Cottage for the summer.'

'How on earth did you — ' She didn't even bother finishing the question, already knowing the answer. Jasper had connections everywhere, in the highest levels of society, and if he wanted to find out where someone was, he would. 'Have you been checking up on me?'

'Let's call it checking in. I owe it to Finn.'

'Well, you don't owe *me* anything.'

'You still hate me, don't you?' Jasper adjusted the peak of his cap so that he could fix her with his famous stare, and she shook her head slowly.

'I don't hate you, I hate what happened to Finn, and I hate you for introducing him to a life that ended up with him dead on a beach halfway across the world.'

'Don't think I haven't thought about that myself, but Finn died doing what he loved. He was always a risk taker; you'd never have opened the restaurant in London if he hadn't been, but you were the anchor he always wanted to come home to.'

'Until he didn't.' She wiped a tear away with the back of her hand, annoyed with herself for crying in front of Jasper.

'He wouldn't want you to bury yourself down here, living a half-life. I saw the way you watched Elliott Dorton getting into the lifeboat. I've seen that look before, Anna, and I recognise an irresistible pull between two people when I see it. Even if I've never felt it myself.'

'Your trouble is that you feel an irresistible pull to every attractive woman you meet, Jasper. Until the next one comes along, that is.'

'Harsh, but true. The real thing is very rare, though. The question is, are you going to act on things with Elliott?'

'How do you even know who he is?'

'One of the reasons I moved down here was because of his centre's growing reputation. I want to pack as much adventure into life as I can, when I'm not filming. I have so many clauses in my contracts now to prevent accidents and injury disrupting filming and costing the studios money — when I'm not working, I want to try everything I can. I had my assistant do some research on the sort of activities that were available in the local area when I saw the house in Figgy Bay, and Elliott Dorton's place is one of Port Kara's biggest selling points. I got a small private beach with the house when I bought it, but the surf on the main beach is what draws everyone here, including me. Plus, there are paparazzi constantly lurking near the beach at my place almost all the time. But even if I want to use the main beach, I have to hide behind the beard and hat, so I look like everyone else. Although maybe not everyone . . . Take

Elliott, for example; he's in a different league, looks-wise.' He paused and fixed her with his stare again. 'How do *you* know him? I never had you down as the adventurous type, even before Finn's accident.'

'He rescued Albie from a cliff edge after he ran off and we just sort of became friends.' She wasn't going to tell him about her volunteering at the adventure centre. She didn't want to give Jasper any more ammunition. Fixing her up with Elliott would have suited him down to the ground. It would have eased his conscience to think she was moving on, just like he'd been able to do so easily. Jasper had been with Finn on that fateful surfing trip, and he'd been one of the friends to perform CPR, and the first person to offer Anna support — financially and otherwise. But when everyone, including Jasper, just carried on with their lives after the funeral, she was the one left behind.

'I saw the two of you walking along

the beach together when I was coming out of the surf. Even Albie seemed to approve.'

'We both like Elliott, with an emphasis on the word *like*. But we're going home in a few weeks and, even if I wasn't, I'm not ready for a new relationship.'

'Who said anything about a *relationship*?' Jasper roared with laughter, turning a few heads on the beach as he did. He lowered his voice, clearly realising he might be about to reveal himself to the dreaded autograph-hunters. 'What you need is a fling. Everyone knows that you can't have two serious relationships in a row, if you want the second one to work. You're still too hung-up on relationship number one to be ready for another Mr Right. You just need a Mr Right Now.'

'Says the man who's only ever looking for Miss Right Now; or should that be Miss Right This Minute?'

'Okay, so I might not be a relationship expert, but I'm an old man. I know what I'm talking about.'

'You're not old. You're not even sixty yet.'

'Yes, but like Finn always said, you only get one life, and I'm making the most of mine, especially now that the years seem to be going by so quickly. Go out and grab yours; make Elliott your Mr Right Now. You'll thank me in the end, when you meet someone else you can build a life with, and I don't think Elliott will have any complaints either.'

'Don't use what Finn said against me.'

'Don't get defensive when you know I'm right, then.' Jasper held up his hands. 'Look, in the end, it's up to you, but I just don't want you to be lonely.'

'I'm fine, I've got Albie and — '

'You can't finish that sentence, can you?' Jasper didn't even wait for her to answer. 'Why don't you come to the house? We can have a dinner party like we used to, in the old days. I won't even make you cook.'

'Nothing is like it was in the old

days.' Anna turned back towards Myrtle Cottage. 'I'll see you around, Jasper.' Walking away from him, she didn't turn back, even when he called out her name. All she needed was Albie, whatever Jasper thought. She just hoped she'd be able to walk away from Elliott as easily, when the time came. However much she tried to hold back from him, though, she still couldn't stop thinking about that accidental kiss, or shake off the voice in her head that was repeating Finn's favourite phrase. You only get one life, and she didn't want to waste it.

6

Elliott had barely had a chance to talk to Anna since he'd taken her to the lifeboat station, but he'd decided not to quiz her about what the other crew members had said anyway. If Jonty had given away his secret, and told Anna how he really felt, then he was better off not asking. He was pretty sure she felt the same attraction to him, as he did to her, but somewhere along the line they'd made an unspoken pact to ignore it. They both had good enough reason. He didn't want to make it awkward between them and the longer they went without speaking, the harder it was going to be to act like he didn't know what she was talking about, if she mentioned something Jonty had said.

They could always stick to the safe ground of talking about the centre, though. So two days before the big

143

event for Going Dutch, Elliott walked into the kitchen to check on Anna's progress with the event, and get some feedback on how the current week's agency chef was getting on. She didn't even look up, she was so engrossed in showing Billy how to create tempered chocolate cylinders on what looked like sheets of acetate. It was one of the items on the menu for the beach party. The contact from Going Dutch had said they wanted trestle tables set up on the patch of private beach that belonged to the adventure centre. It would either be a disaster or a game-changer, but with Anna providing the menu, his money was on the latter.

She was so focussed on Billy's progress, and the young chef was hanging onto her every word. She had no idea the effect she had on the people she came into contact with, and for the hundredth time he wished he could have known her before she was widowed, and before she'd met Finn.

'Right, I think I've got it.' Billy

grinned, both of them still seemingly unaware that Elliott was there.

'Why don't you have a go, then? Once we've got enough cylinders, we can start on the chocolate orange mousse filling.' Anna turned away as Billy began spreading the chocolate over the acetate, and suddenly caught sight of Elliott.

'I didn't see you there! You made me jump.'

'Sorry, I just didn't want to interrupt you by saying anything.' She had a smear of chocolate on her cheek, and the desire to kiss it off almost overwhelmed him. This wasn't getting any easier.

'That's okay. Billy's doing a grand job. Sadly I can't say the same for the agency chef. He went out for his lunch hour two hours ago and he hasn't come back yet. He knows how busy we are, too.'

'I take it we haven't found our new head chef yet, then?'

'I'm afraid not. I just wish we had a

bit longer. If I had a few months, I could easily train Billy up to head chef level, he's got so much potential.' The young sous chef's cheeks blazed with colour as she spoke, but he was still wearing a grin like a Cheshire cat.

'I wish you had longer, too. Sorry.' Elliott gave her an apologetic shrug as his phone began to ring. There was no point telling her that there were far more reasons he wished she could stay than just training Billy. 'I better take this call.'

Pushing open the back door of the kitchen to the courtyard behind it, where Anna had started planting up a herb garden, he answered the call from an unknown number.

'Hello, Elliott Dorton speaking.'

'Ah, so you answer your phone from unknown numbers, but not from your father?' Charles Dorton had a distinctive tone, which always made it sound like he was giving Elliott a lecture. And he usually was.

'I've been busy.'

'I left you three messages.'

'I know.'

'And I suppose you haven't had a chance to return any of those calls?'

'I was waiting for the right moment.' Elliott didn't add that there was no such thing, as far as he was concerned. Speaking to his dad could always wait.

'Did you listen to the messages?'

'Not all the way through.'

'I guessed you hadn't. Otherwise you'd have called.' His father's tone was clipped; there was never any hint of affection, so what Charles said next almost knocked him off his feet. 'I've read some of the reviews for that centre of yours, there was a big piece in The Guardian last week. It seems to be doing pretty well.'

'We're doing okay.'

'How much money are you making?' His father's question was far less of a surprise, it was the bottom line that never changed.

'Like I said, we're doing okay.'

'Have you spoken to your mother?'

147

'Not this week. Have you?' He felt a stab of guilt. Elliott and his mother were both busy, but he knew he should find more time to check in on her and make sure she was okay — although he had no idea why his father was asking. He'd barely seemed to care when he'd been married to her, let alone now.

'I haven't spoken to her either, but you're going to have to call her after this. Chantel and I are getting married, and I want you to tell your mother.'

'You're doing what?' Elliott could try to convince himself he didn't care what his father did any more, but the idea that he was marrying his former personal assistant, who was two years younger than Elliott, when she was so clearly only after his precious money, was ridiculous. But there was worse still to come.

'She's having a baby. We got a private scan this week and it's a boy. So this is my second chance to raise a son who wants to follow in my footsteps.'

'He'll be pushing you around in a

wheelchair by the time he turns eighteen.' Elliott could taste the bitterness. His father was sixty-eight, thirty-five years older than his new fiancée. But if she was just a gold-digger, as Elliott suspected, then they deserved each other.

'So you'll call your mother?'

'I doubt she'll care.'

'That's the problem, though, isn't it? If either of you had ever cared what I wanted, the family would still be together, and I wouldn't have to be starting again in my sixties.'

'Are you for real?'

'All I wanted was a supportive wife and a son who would follow in my footsteps.'

'I tried and so did Mum.' Elliott didn't want to listen to his father's response. 'I'll talk to her because I think she deserves to know, not because you asked me to. Goodbye.'

Ending the call, he stared at the phone for a moment, fighting the urge to throw it over the kitchen garden wall and into the sea beyond.

'Are you okay?' Anna tentatively opened the kitchen door and stepped out into the courtyard, letting it close behind her. 'I thought I heard raised voices.'

'You did. I was arguing with my father again.'

'I'm sorry, it's none of my business.' She turned back towards the door again, but he reached out and gently caught hold of her wrist. He needed to talk to someone and he wanted it to be Anna.

'I hate the fact that he can make me feel like an eight year old again and that I'm a constant source of disappointment, but he just has this uncanny knack of doing it every time we speak.' Elliott was still holding her wrist and she took a step towards him.

'For what it's worth, I think he's jealous. He must see this life you've built for yourself, following your passion, and wonder how he let everything he does revolve around money. Deep down, I bet he misses you too.' Her voice was so gentle that he couldn't help leaning his body towards hers, and she didn't move away.

'He's got a funny way of showing it. He only rang to tell me that he's marrying the woman he left mum for and that they're having a little boy. He couldn't wait to tell me how much he's looking forward to having a son who'll finally live up to his hopes.'

'Not realising how amazing you are is his loss.' Anna tilted her head towards him and he gently kissed her forehead, before forcing himself to pull away again.

'You're the amazing one.'

'I — ' He watched her mouth, but she'd stopped talking and, despite all the things he'd told himself about what a disaster it would be to get involved with her, in the end he couldn't stop himself. The sweet, flowery notes of her perfume filled the air between them, and he could feel her breath on his skin as he pulled her towards him again. This time, when their lips met, it was no accident. The kiss was hesitant at first; he wanted to make sure that she wanted this as much as him, but suddenly his hands were in her hair, her body pressed up against him, and weeks of longing passed like an electric current between them.

'I've been wanting to do that since that first moment on the cliffside.' Elliott was the first to speak as they finally pulled apart. He'd half expected Anna to tell him that it was another accident, another mistake they shouldn't have made, but her eyes were sparkling, like they did when she laughed. Anna opened her mouth to answer him, just as Billy flung open the door from the kitchen, making them spring apart — the spell was instantly broken.

'You'll never guess who owns Going Dutch?' Billy was virtually dancing on the spot, but Elliott couldn't have attempted to guess even if he wanted to. After that kiss he was barely thinking straight; all he could think about was Anna.

'If we're never going to guess, you

better just tell us!' Anna laughed and Elliott had to force himself to drag his eyes away from her mouth to look at Billy. How could she manage to act so normal, when he was wondering if he'd ever be the same again?

'It's Jasper Holland! *Going Dutch* and *Holland*, get it?' Billy still couldn't keep still.

'It doesn't get much more high-profile than that.' Elliott turned to Anna, and all the colour seemed to have drained from her face. He had a horrible feeling that the realisation of what they'd done, when they'd crossed that invisible line between them, had just hit her. Whatever it was, she looked utterly miserable.

'No it doesn't, which means we'd better get on with getting the menu ready. The reviews from this could make or break the centre.' She spoke directly to Billy, not turning to look at Elliott again, and two seconds later they'd both disappeared back into the kitchen. He hadn't imagined the way she'd reacted, she'd wanted the kiss every bit as much as he had. So why had she disappeared at the first opportunity she got?

★ ★ ★

Anna had considered leaving Port Kara altogether when she'd heard that it was Jasper Holland who was behind the big beach party. The last thing she wanted was to bump into any more of the old crowd of celebrities who had hung out in the restaurant she'd run with Finn. It had terrified her at first, taking on so much debt to set up the business that her husband had always had so much faith in. Then, when they'd got their first Michelin star, it had all gone crazy. They went from waiting for the phone to ring, and praying that they'd have enough bookings to fill the restaurant on a Friday and Saturday night, to having a waiting list every night of the week. Of course, if you had the right name, you could always bag a table, and the restaurant had a list of celebrity clientele that any showbiz agent would have given their right arm for. Jasper Holland had been a regular and he'd soon become fast friends with Finn, who was a natural at networking and never seemed fazed, no matter how high-profile their latest celebrity diner was. Anna had always preferred to stay behind the scenes, working in the kitchen and doing what she loved best. It was why they'd been the perfect partnership from the moment they'd met, when she was just nineteen. But everything from back then reminded her of Finn and she didn't want to see any of the old faces, not now.

Her mouth had felt bruised from the passion of kissing Elliott and she'd been sure in that moment that she was ready to move on. He wasn't looking for anything serious, he lived for the adventure centre, but she'd come to the conclusion that maybe Jasper was right, and that she needed something where there were no expectations, to bridge the gap between her marriage to Finn and being ready to think about something serious. Elliott seemed to fit the bill perfectly and, when he'd kissed her, she'd felt a surge of desire stronger than anything she'd ever felt, even with Finn. She'd swallowed down the guilt when the comparison had popped into her head. She couldn't bring Finn back, any more than she could change what she'd felt, when she'd been enveloped in Elliott's arms. There were just some things in life you couldn't control, and it turned out that having the past come crashing back into your present was one of them.

In the end, she'd decided she wasn't going to let Jasper Holland's decisions have that much impact on her life for a second time. She was staying in Port Kara until September as she'd planned but had no intention whatsoever to attend the party Jasper was throwing in person. The event had been planned as a joint stag and hen do for Jasper's godson, who also happened to be a second cousin of the Queen, and his fiancée. So everybody from the centre wanted to volunteer to wait tables or serve drinks at the event. Anna had designed the menu as a very posh picnic and had done her bit by preparing all of the food in advance, alongside Billy and one of the agency chefs. Elliott was taking the hen and stag party out for a series of activities, which included the opportunity to try out paragliding, as well as the slightly less terrifying option of zorbing. Then they'd all be returning for the picnic on the centre's private beach, as the paparazzi were apparently still permanently camped out by the private beach at Jasper's new house.

There were more agency staff, and one of the other sous chefs who went to college with Billy, covering the evening service at the centre itself. Anna had taken Albie for a walk up to the centre to check on their progress and make sure that everyone was okay. Deciding to walk back along the new coastal path had been a whim, and she'd barely even thought about the fact that it would take her right past the centre's private beach, where Elliott and the others would be working hard to make sure Jasper's party went off without a hitch.

She was far enough away not to be spotted, but she could see the two long picnic tables that had been set up, side by side, like something you might see at a family wedding in Italy. Jasper was sitting at the head of one of the tables and his raucous laugh carried up to Anna, on the gentle summer breeze. If Finn had been around, he'd have been down there amongst the partygoers for sure. Not because he had any particular fascination with the royal family, especially not distant cousins of the Queen, but because he always liked to be at the centre of what was going on. Scanning the group on the beach, Anna tried to see if there was anyone else she recognised, as Albie stuck his nose into a patch of reed, and started to dig.

She couldn't see Elliott at first. There were a few faces she recognised from

TV and magazine covers, and some of them had been regulars at the restaurant too. But he wasn't sitting amongst the guests, even though she was sure Jasper would have invited him to. That was another difference between Finn and Elliott. They were both driven, but Elliott definitely wanted the business to take the spotlight, rather than wanting to make sure he was noticed.

'Come on, boy, let's get going.' Anna pulled gently on Albie's lead, to get him to lift his head out of the reeds. 'We can't stay up here all day.' She felt self-conscious, suddenly, like the only kid not invited to a birthday party, pressing their nose up against the window.

Pulling a reluctant Albie behind her, she carried on along the coastal path, to the point where there was a crossroads, giving you the option of either heading down the slope to the private beach, or up across the cliff towards another path that led down to the main beach in Port Kara. Just as she reached the crossroads, she heard a scream. Glancing down, she could see what looked like half the partygoers running towards the edge of the water and, at first, she assumed the screams were excitement, fuelled by too much champagne and a group decision to head into the water to carry on the fun.

'He's drowning!' A woman shouted the words, her voice high, bordering on the hysterical, but no-one seemed to be reacting. Looking further out, she could see a man in the waves, his arms flailing as he tried to keep his head above the water. Then she saw Elliott, running full pelt towards the sea and diving in to the left of the crowd. He was moving through the water quickly, and seconds later he'd reached the man, whose arms didn't stop flailing even when Elliott got to him and began swimming back to the shore. Anna could hardly breathe, her mind racing between the present and the past. Had someone swum out to Finn like that? Nothing could change what had happened to him, and all she wanted now was to see Elliott and the other man emerge from the water and be okay.

'Come on.' She whispered the words, her hands involuntarily moving together, almost as if she was saying a prayer. Dropping the lead, along with her concentration, Albie seized the opportunity to taste freedom and shot down the path towards the private beach, before she even had a second to react.

'Albie, no!'

Chasing after him, she almost tripped, as her eyes kept darting towards the group of people still standing on the edge of the water, watching Elliott's slow progress towards the shore. What was wrong with them? Why wasn't anyone helping him?

Albie was much quicker than her, and he was on the beach and thundering toward the crowd before she was even halfway down. It was a miracle that he'd run past the abandoned picnic and hadn't just taken the opportunity to help himself to all that unattended food. But he was making a beeline towards the water and no amount of shouting on Anna's part seemed to be having any impact.

She was breathless by the time her trainer-clad feet hit the sand and, looking up, she could see that Albie had gone into the water. Unlike most Labradors, he usually preferred keeping his paws on dry land, but not today. Within seconds he was far enough out to start swimming and he drew level with Elliott just as Anna finally reached the edge of the crowd, who were all still just watching, even as she started to wade into the water.

Albie circled Elliott and the other man, who finally seemed to have stopped fighting his rescuer. But he wasn't moving at all and that seemed much worse from where Anna was standing. Turning back to face the beach, Albie took hold of the man's shirt in his mouth and began pulling him in the same direction that Elliott was swimming, and at last the crowd started to react.

'Get back onto the beach, Anna, it's

okay.' Elliott looked up in response to the noise of the crowd, shouting the instruction to her, and she hesitated for a moment before doing as she was told.

'Look at that dog, he's saving Rory!' A woman's voice in the crowd was incredulous.

'I told him not to go in after necking that bottle of champagne. Thank heavens for Elliott.' It was a man's voice this time.

'I would have given him a hand,' someone else said, sounding like he was trying to convince himself as much as the crowd around him, 'but he said I'd probably be more of a hindrance than a help.'

'Shall we call an ambulance?' Another woman turned towards Jasper, who shook his head.

'Let's see how they are first.' Jasper said, and Anna knew the score. He was trying to avoid the negative publicity, if he could. It was bad enough that he'd been associated with Finn's death, and how much of that had been plastered all over the press. His name associated with another near-drowning was the last thing Jasper, or his agent, would want.

Anna ran towards Elliott as he dragged the man on to the beach, Albie still pulling on his shirt.

'Is he okay?'

'He will be.' Elliott turned the man's head to one side, and water began to drain out of his mouth straight away. Suddenly, he was coughing up more water, and the colour immediately seemed to come back into his face as he took in big gasps of air. 'Keep breathing, Rory, and don't try to say anything yet.'

'Do we need an ambulance?' Jasper didn't seem to notice Anna as he asked the question, and Elliott nodded.

'We should get him checked over, just in case. I don't think he ever really lost consciousness, but he's swallowed quite a bit of water.'

'Any chance that just being seen by a doctor would suffice? I can get my private guy down here by helicopter in twenty minutes if needs be.'

'It might be quicker in that case. He's not a high-category emergency and the ambulance almost certainly wouldn't get here that quickly.' As Elliott answered, Rory sat up, almost as if to emphasise that this wasn't an emergency.

'I'm fine to go back to the party.'

'No, you're not.' Elliott's tone didn't broker an argument and Rory slowly nodded his head. 'We'll get you up to the centre to wait for the doctor, whilst Jasper puts in the call.'

'Can we do it at my place instead? It'll help keep things low-key.' Jasper suddenly noticed Anna and smiled, but she didn't respond. Had he tried to hush up Finn's death in the same way?

'I'll get a couple of the lads to bring a stretcher down and we can move him up to the centre. If he seems well enough to be moved again when we get up there, I'll get one of the lads to drive him down to your place. If you can give your doctor a call, to make sure he can get here, I'll give the centre a ring.'

'Are you okay?' Anna dropped down

to her knees on the sand beside Elliott, as Jasper disappeared to make the call.

'I was flagging until Albie stepped in.' Elliott grinned as he checked Rory's pulse, the other man's breathing getting far less laboured with every breath.

'The pair of you scared me half to death.'

'I'm sorry.' He let go of Rory's wrist and took hold of her hand. 'That must have been hard for you, after what happened to Finn. But I'm okay and so is Albie, even Rory here is going to be alright. Although him going into the water like that, with so much alcohol on board, was really stupid.' Rory mumbled an apology that neither of them acknowledged.

'I couldn't bear for it to happen again, that's why — ' She didn't even get the chance to finish the sentence and explain why she'd backed off after they'd kissed, as difficult as that had been. There was no room in her life for another risk-taker.

'My doctor's on his way; he'll be here

by six at the latest.' Jasper cut her off and Elliott nodded.

'I'll give a couple of the lads a call to bring the stretcher down, and I'll drive Rory to your place if he's up to it. Are you coming?' For a moment, Anna thought Elliott was talking to her.

'I'll meet you there. You'll be alright until then, won't you Rory.' Jasper ruffled the other man's hair, like he might have done to Albie.

'Can I come and see you later?' This time Elliott was definitely talking to Anna, and she hated the fact that Jasper was watching them.

'What for?'

'I need to bring this hero a big steak to thank him for helping me get Rory in safely.' Elliott bent down and patted Albie's head.

'Okay.'

'I'll see you later then.'

'Uh, huh.' Anna wasn't going to say any more than she had to, not while all the time she could sense that Jasper was still watching her. As Elliott walked away to call the centre and to get the other guides down on to the beach, some of the partygoers started to crowd around Rory. They were even taking selfies, now that the drama was over.

'He could be your stepping stone, you know.' Jasper's tone was determined.

'What?' Anna was already walking away in the direction of Myrtle Cottage, as Jasper drew level with her.

'You know, the stepping stone between what you had with Finn and your next serious relationship. Like I said before, he's perfect for the job.'

'The *job*?' She tried to laugh, but it was more of a choking sound. 'I'm not looking for a relationship or a stepping stone, as you so eloquently put it.'

'You don't have to be looking. Sometimes these things find you and it's a good idea not to pass them by when they do. After all, you only get one life.'

'Don't you dare throw that back at me again!' She was walking more quickly now, Albie having to trot to keep up.

'Don't let this chance to move on slip away, then.'

'Goodbye, Jasper.' It was the second time she hadn't stuck around to hear him out and she'd almost broken into a run by now, so she didn't hear what Jasper said next. He had no idea how much she wanted to act on her feelings for Elliott, but it was too much of a risk. Not just because Elliott liked nothing better than dicing with danger, but because she was almost certain that her feelings for him couldn't be kept casual. Either way, he'd end up breaking her heart and she'd only just started to piece it back together.

★ ★ ★

It was getting dark by the time Elliott walked down the path to Myrtle Cottage. Albie jumped up at the front window and started barking as soon as he saw him. That dog was amazing; not only did he leap into the sea to rescue drowning men, but he could also smell rump steak from nearly twenty feet away. Anna was already at the door by the time he got to it, the soft glow of the lamp on the wall outside highlighting her silhouette. She was wearing a plum-coloured jumper that clung to her body and looked like it would have been soft to the touch — almost as soft as the long blonde hair that hung loosely over her shoulders.

'How was Rory?' Anna moved slightly to one side to let him in, and he breathed in the distinctive scent of her floral perfume. He couldn't remember ever being as attracted to anyone else as he was to her, and after what Jasper had revealed about her, she was all the more fascinating.

'He's fine. Jasper's doctor gave him the all clear and, last I saw, he was lying on a chaise longue in one of the rooms at Jasper's place that overlooks the sea, being fussed over by at least three beautiful women.'

'*Beautiful* women?'

'Most people would probably say so,

but I've seen better.'

'Really?'

'Definitely.' They were in danger of moving into unknown territory, but she didn't seem to be pushing him away in the way that she usually did. He needed to talk to her about what Jasper had told him, though. 'How's Albie? Has he recovered from his swim?'

'As you can see, he's fine, and I think he knows what you've got for him!' Anna laughed as Albie continued to weave himself in and out of Elliott's legs. 'I think we ought to put him out of his misery and let him have what he wants, don't you?'

'Absolutely.' Elliott only wished it was as easy for him. What he wanted was standing in front of him, so close that he could reach out and touch her. But it wasn't as simple as that.

'Can I get you a drink?' Anna said, taking the bag of steak from him, and putting some of it in Albie's bowl.

'Yes, please; that would be great, if I'm not holding you up.'

'Nope, it's just me and Albie, with no plans except to watch a bit of trashy reality TV later. Same as always.'

'Why?'

'Why what?'

'Why don't you have other plans? Not just for tonight, but everything.' He looked at her levelly for a moment. 'Jasper told me some things.'

'I bet he did.' Anna turned away from him and opened the door of the fridge. 'Wine or beer?'

'Beer would be good, thanks.' He could feel the tension in the air as he took the bottle from her. 'I'm sorry, the last thing I want to do is to upset you.'

'It's okay, but if you're going to hear everything, you might as well hear it from me.' Anna took a bottle of white wine from the fridge and picked up a glass. 'Let's go through to the sitting room and I'll tell you all about it.'

The curtain of darkness outside the cottage seemed to have closed in at the same time as Anna had shut the front door behind him. It was a clear night and the stars that lit up the sky outside the sitting room window reminded him yet again why he loved Port Kara so much. He'd never seen a sky that big or that clear when he'd spent all his time in London, and by the end he felt hemmed in there, to the point where he felt he could barely breathe. There were rows of solar lights strung across the front garden of Myrtle Cottage, trying to compete with the stars, and he knew right at that moment that he could have stayed there forever.

'So, what did Jasper tell you?' Anna poured herself a glass of wine as she spoke, and he wondered how much he should say. But if they were laying their cards on the table, then it was time to be honest.

'He asked me how I felt about snagging a Michelin-starred chef.'

'I should have told you.'

'I'm surprised you didn't, but it's up to you which bits of your past life you want to share, and who you want to share them with.' Elliott frowned.

'Although I must have looked pretty confused, as I had no idea what he was talking about. Especially when he called you Annabelle Douglas-Jones.'

'That's my married name and my real first name is Annabelle, but my friends have always called me Anna, anyway. But the truth is, I didn't want to be that person and everything that's associated with that, whilst I'm down here.'

'If I had a Michelin star, I'd get a wardrobe full of t-shirts made advertising it, and wear one every day, so everyone would know how brilliant I was!' Elliott laughed, trying to ease some of the tension, but Anna was shaking her head.

'No, you wouldn't. The Douglas-Jones brand was really Finn's, anyway. He got his Michelin star before me and it was that that drove customers to Casa Cibo.'

'But you were the youngest chef ever to get a Michelin star. I bet Marco Pierre-White hates you for knocking him off that spot.'

'You googled me, didn't you?' Anna pulled a face. 'I never wanted all of that notoriety, I was happiest hidden away in the kitchen, doing what I loved.'

'Nothing much has changed, has it?' He took a sip of his beer. 'So why did you tell me you were a sous chef?'

'I was, to all intents and purposes, second-in-command to Finn. He was the figurehead, the one who was happy to hang out with the customers and make Casa Cibo more than a place to eat. It was Finn who the celebrity clientele came to spend time with, and that's how we got to know Jasper so well.'

'And you never resented that?' Elliott decided not to tell her what Jasper had said, about how keen Finn had been to become a celebrity in his own right, but something flickered across Anna's eyes.

'We were a good partnership and, like I said, I wasn't interested in any of that. Jasper was the one who got Finn into adventure sport, and it was Jasper who was with him when he died. But I guess you know that if you googled me.'

'I didn't google you. Jasper told me about you being the youngest recipient of the Michelin star.'

'Right.' Anna took a deep breath. 'Well if you google Annabelle Douglas-Jones, you'll see the whole story and you'll understand why I wanted to be just plain Anna Turner down here. That's who I was until I met Finn, and it's who I needed to be again — at least for the summer whilst I work out who I am without him.'

'Do you blame Jasper?' Elliott watched Anna's face as she seemed to consider his question for a moment and then finally shake her head.

'No . . . at least not anymore. I did and sometimes I have, because it's easier to pin the blame on someone and have something to lash out at, than to accept it's a freak accident that could have happened to anyone. If that's the case, then why did it have to happen to me?'

'I'm sorry — '

'I know you are. Everyone is.' She shook her head again. 'But that's not it. The accident was always going to be covered in the press, because Jasper was there and Finn had become quite well known in his own right, but then things went crazy.'

'You don't have to tell me if you don't want to. And I promise not to google it, if you don't want to tell me.' He meant it, too, and it was a promise he was determined to keep, no matter how curious he might be. He hated the thought of anyone or anything hurting Anna, and he wasn't going to be part of that.

'Do you know what? I believe you, and that's exactly why I'm going to tell you.' She took another sip of wine. 'After the accident, two women came forward and said they were with Finn and Jasper in their hotel suite the night before the accident.'

'Oh no, how awful.'

'There were both underwear models,

so you can imagine how that made things look. They were trying to make a name for themselves and so it seemed too good an opportunity to miss.'

'So they were lying?'

'Not exactly. They were in Jasper's suite, with him, *both* of them were — but Finn wasn't there.'

'Right.'

'Do you hear that doubt in your voice? That's exactly how everyone sounded and what everyone else thought, especially after all the coverage it got in the press.'

'Sorry — ' He seemed to be making a habit of saying that.

'Don't be, you didn't know Finn like I did, and I know he'd never have done that to me. Much as he liked to court the celebrity lifestyle, I was his one and only, and I never doubted that for a moment, not even after the story broke. But even if I'd had any doubts, Jasper would have set me straight. He told me the truth straight away and he even arranged it with his PR for the two girls to sell the true story of what went on with him that night, to one of the tabloids. But by then the damage was done and mine and Finn's marriage was tainted in the eyes of everyone else. The original story still appears if you google either of our names, or look up Casa Cibo, and I wanted to leave all of that behind.'

'I can understand that. Sometimes you have to reinvent yourself to move on.' Elliott's escape from the past might not have been quite so dramatic, but he'd been every bit as keen to leave it behind him and make a fresh start.

'We're a pair aren't we?' Anna smiled.

'Are we?' Elliott couldn't help asking the question. He wanted them to be something, he was more certain of that than ever, but he didn't know what they *could* be. Not when she was leaving so soon. What Jasper had told him had changed the game, though. He might have omitted to mention what had happened with the two models in his hotel suite, but Jasper changed the Elliott looked at Anna. She wasn't a fragile widow, who needed treating with kid gloves, she was a survivor and a success — a huge success — but somehow completely devoid of ego at the same time. That was something almost as rare as it was attractive. Anna Turner, Annabelle Douglas-Jones, or whatever she chose to call herself, she was something special.

'I like you, Elliott.'

'You *like* me?'

'I'm not looking for any more than that.' She topped up her glass and looked across at him. 'Jasper's opinion is not usually something I set a lot of store by; he spends so much time acting that I sometimes wonder if he knows what's real anymore. But the last couple of times I've spoken to him, he actually said something that made sense.'

'And what was that?'

'He said that I should let myself date again; take a few baby steps towards having another proper relationship.'

Anna bit her bottom lip, and it was all he could do not to cross the room and kiss her again. 'And I wondered if we should, you know, try it?'

'Dating?' Elliott definitely wanted to spend more time with Anna, but he wasn't sure if he wanted to be the guy who helped her get ready for her next proper relationship.

'We're attracted to each other and we already know that we can pull off a pretty good kiss.' She smiled, suddenly shy. 'But I'm a city girl, who'll be going home at the end of the summer, and you're a workaholic who can't bear to be out of sight of the sea. So we'd never work, even if the timing was right. We could be something to each other, though, even if that's just a great way to spend the rest of the summer.'

'Do you think it'll be that easy to stop ourselves from getting in too deep?' Every time he looked at Anna, he was less and less sure he could keep her at arm's length, but she seemed certain.

'We want different things, so it couldn't ever work long term. But I really like you, Elliott, and I don't want to regret not taking this chance.' She raised an eyebrow. 'You're supposed to be the risk-taker, after all.'

'I really like you, too.' Something was holding Elliott back, but it was stupid. He'd never been in love in his life, so why he thought it might happen with Anna he didn't know. She was right, though; living with regret was no way to live. They might go on two dates and decide that it had all been a horrible mistake, or they might have the best few weeks imaginable. Either way, he'd be able to get Anna out of his system and move on — go back to concentrating on the one thing he did love, his business. 'Do you think Albie will accept me?'

'Oh, I think he likes you even more than I do.' Anna giggled again, as Albie laid his head on Elliott's knee, looking up at him with total adoration as he always did.

'Well, I guess that's decided then.' Gently lifting the dog's head off his knee, Elliott stood up and finally crossed the room. 'Do you have a rule about kissing on a first date?'

'Is this a date?'

'It can be if you want it to be.'

'Then, yes. I do have a rule, which absolutely cannot be broken.' Reaching up to touch the side of his face, she slid her hand into his hair, pulling him closer to her, until their lips met with that same passionate intensity as they had before. He was determined to live in the moment and enjoy every second he got to spend with Anna. The end of the summer was still a long way off and anything could happen before then.

7

Moving their relationship beyond friendship to something that Elliott couldn't really label had been less of a choice than an unstoppable urge, in the end. Every time Anna was in the same room, his eyes were drawn to her and he couldn't believe it wasn't obvious to everyone that something was going on between them. But if Billy and the others had any idea what was going on, they were keeping it to themselves. It suited him and Anna, though. They'd gone into whatever this relationship was without any expectations, so having to deal with the expectations of anyone else was something they could do without. It was hard enough to grab time together; the centre was busier than ever, and they still hadn't found a permanent member of staff to take over as head chef.

His suspicion that it would be almost

impossible to replace Anna had proved correct, but Billy was making huge progress under her tutelage, so Elliott had felt able to leave him in charge of the kitchen, supervising some agency staff, for two days when the centre finally had less guests booked than usual. A company that had been sending its staff on an overnight team-building session had gone into liquidation almost overnight, which left the centre at half-occupancy. Never one to miss an opportunity, Elliott asked Anna if they could take a road trip, to check out new local suppliers for the restaurant, and add a more authentic Cornish taste to the dishes they offered on the menu.

Anna had said she'd come along if Albie could make the trip too, and they were going to visit suppliers of everything from locally caught crab to Cornish yarg, a semi-hard cheese that was wrapped in stinging nettles. Elliott had booked lunch for them in Finbar Bay, which was a quirky little town, stacked high on a hillside above the harbour where the best crab in Cornwall was brought in fresh every day. He'd wondered if Anna would resent the fact that they were spending the time they'd managed to snatch together checking out suppliers, but she'd seemed really excited by the prospect, and if he was honest, he just wanted to spend time with her. He had a feeling she'd have turned him down if he'd suggested a romantic break somewhere; she was still holding back so much of herself. But what she offered was enough for him. He was holding back bits of himself, too, after all.

'If I'd known Albie was dressing up for the occasion, I'd have made more of an effort.' Elliott opened the back door of the car, to let the dog jump in. Albie was wearing a red and white spotted bandana collar, his tail thumping heavily against the back rest of the seat, as Elliott closed the door.

'You look pretty good to me.' Anna grinned.

'Not as good as you.' He opened the passenger side door for her, the pale blue and white striped dress she was wearing showing just a hint of toned thigh as she got into the car.

'I didn't know if I should wear something a bit warmer; they've forecast a big storm, but we should be home by then.'

'It'll be fine, the storms here always seem to hit overnight.' Elliott closed the door and walked around to his side of the car. They weren't staying out together overnight; it was another unspoken agreement between them. And for Elliott, it was self-preservation.

'So, where are we going first?' Anna turned to him as he started the car, and Albie stuck his head through the gap between their seats.

'We're going to a dairy farm about twenty miles inland. They apparently won a world cheese championship for their Cornish yarg.' Elliott pulled a face. 'I had no idea there even was a world cheese championship.'

'Then you haven't lived.' Anna laughed as Elliott pulled onto the road that led out of Port Kara. There was no one else he'd rather have been spending a rare day out of the centre with, and the conversation flowed easily between them as they drove along the twisting country lanes that took them further inland.

A cow poked its head over a stone wall as they pulled into the farmyard at the dairy. The buildings, crafted from grey stone, were arranged in a horse-shoe shape, and the longest of the low barns had obviously been converted into a farm shop at some point. There was a sign directing visitors to the holiday cottage complex, which was housed in more converted buildings beyond the main farmyard, and Elliott couldn't help wishing that he could spend a whole week there with Anna. Whether he found another chef or not, she'd have to leave Port Kara by the end of the third week of September at the latest. Every time he turned over the schedule where they wrote up all of the centre's events to a new day, he tried not to think about how quickly the summer was galloping past.

'It's lovely here.' Anna stepped out of the car at the same time as him. 'But I think we'd better leave Alb in the car as it's so much cooler today.'

'I'll leave the windows open a bit.' Elliott lowered the glass in the back windows and locked the car. The wind was definitely starting to pick up and the sky in the distance had taken on a gun-metal grey appearance. The storm might be coming sooner than either of them expected.

'You must be from Dorton Adventure Centre?' The middle-aged woman, who'd crossed the farmyard to meet them, was wearing a bottle-green bodywarmer and a welcoming expression as she thrust out her hand towards them. 'I'm Mary Polton. Welcome to Polton Dairy Farm, home of the world-championship-winning yarg.'

'Pleased to meet you.' Elliott caught

Anna's eye as he shook Mary's hand, and he could see she was trying not to laugh.

'Come in, come in. We've got lots for you to sample and there might be a few other things you want to consider us supplying. Our clotted cream is shipped out all over the world, and we've just won an international award for our clotted cream gin. We'll have more gold medals than Usain Bolt, the rate we're going!'

'I feel like an under-achiever.' Elliott whispered under his breath to Anna, as they followed Mary across the farm-yard, and she grinned in response. He'd had his fair share of girlfriends over the years, but he'd never had a friendship like this with a woman. His attraction to Anna was so much more than physical.

Their host hadn't been exaggerating when she'd said she had lots of things for them to try. He hadn't sampled the clotted cream gin because he was driving, but to be fair to Mary Polton, everything else had lived up to the hype she'd given it. Anna had been really enthusiastic about the dishes they could create using not just the yarg and the clotted cream, but the wild garlic, cider and honey that Polton Dairy Farm had also diversified into producing over the years.

'I was thinking that if all the suppliers have as much to offer as this, we could have some weekends where all the produce is exclusively Cornish, and really make it a speciality of the centre.' Anna's face was shining as she spoke, and Elliott loved hearing her say 'we' like that. She had so many ideas for the centre, and so much passion about how the catering side of the business could go, she couldn't really be thinking of leaving, could she?

'That would be fantastic. It's the brand I've always wanted for the centre. Doing activities like coasteering, that fit so well with the location, have always felt quintessentially Cornish to me. Having the rest of the business match with that would be perfect.'

'Do you know, I'm loving this!' Mary Polton clapped her hands together with obvious excitement. 'I only wish my Basil could be here to meet you and hear what you've got to say. You're exactly like we used to be when we were first married and had so many plans for what we wanted to do with the business. It's just brilliant to see a young couple like you two with that same enthusiasm.'

'Oh, we're not — ' As Elliott spoke, Anna held out her hand to stop him, shaking her head.

'You've got an amazing business here. You must be so proud of it.' Anna smiled at Mary. For some reason, she didn't want to put the older woman right, and Elliott was happy to go with it. Whether Mary and Basil realised how lucky they were was the real question. Finding your other half, someone who has the same drive and goals, was something his parents had never achieved. He'd accepted he might not find that himself — there weren't many people who were as passionate about the outdoor life as him, or who wanted to abseil down a cliff-face in a howling wind in November — but it had obviously worked for the Poltons.

'It's taken decades, but we're amazed at what we've achieved when we look back, and never in our wildest dreams did we think we'd end up as world champions!' Mary looked from Anna to Elliott. 'So have I convinced you to use us as a regular supplier?'

'Absolutely.' Anna and Elliott spoke at the same time, and Mary clapped her hands together again.

'See, I knew it; the two of you are totally in sync. Just like me and Basil!'

'Let's talk terms, shall we?' Keen to avoid the conversation making Anna feel uncomfortable, Elliott moved the focus back to business.

Half an hour later, they'd agreed that Polton Dairy Farm would be supplying the centre with several different cheeses, clotted cream, two varieties of gin, cloudy cider, wild garlic and honey. Elliott had even bought some organic dog treats for Albie, which were the only type they sold in the farmshop. They were gluten free, according to Mary, but he doubted Anna's dog would even notice. Albie usually swallowed things whole.

'They had some amazing produce, didn't they?' Elliott turned to look at Anna as they pulled out of the farmyard. As expected, Albie had made short work of his treats and he'd get the chance to stretch his legs and go for a walk on the beach when they got to Finbar Bay.

'Yes, they've built up a brilliant business there. I'd love to do something like that.' There was a slight hint of regret in her voice and he couldn't help wondering if she had more idea of what she was going to do when she got back to London, than she'd had when she first arrived in Port Kara.

'You won't open another restaurant then?'

'I don't think so; I need to do something different. It won't be the same without Finn, and the restaurant was always more his dream than mine. Seeing the Poltons' business, I remembered how much I loved sourcing the produce and creating a taste that is something uniquely authentic. At the restaurant, we tended to run with whatever was on trend, but I love what Mary and Basil are doing.'

'Cornwall would be a great place for you to run a business like that. I know you love London, but surely you can see how much potential there is down here?'

'Maybe.' Anna sighed. 'Thanks for not putting Mary right about us not being married, by the way.'

'No problem.' Elliott hesitated for a moment, wondering whether to ask the obvious question. But in the end he had to. 'Can I ask why you didn't want her to know?'

'Because then I'd probably end up explaining that I was widowed and what had happened to Finn. Sometimes I just don't want to be *that* person. For half an hour, I just wanted to be who Mary thought I was — an excited business owner, with a million plans for how you and I can grow the centre into something we can be incredibly proud of. I was playing pretend, I suppose.'

'I get it.' Elliott took the road towards Finbar Bay and they fell silent, both of them lost in their thoughts. He wanted to say it didn't have to be a pretence, but that would have taken them on to really dangerous ground. Saying it would probably have had Anna packing up her stuff and heading back to London before the week was out. And if it didn't make her do that, what then? Did he really mean it? Was there any chance that people as different as he and Anna clearly were could ever make a relationship work? All the evidence seemed stacked against it and, as she had just pointed out, sometimes it was easier to say nothing at all.

★　★　★

Anna watched the Cornish scenery blurring past the car window, as Elliott drove them towards Finbar Bay. What amazed her about spending time with him was that there were never any awkward silences. They could chat about anything and everything, but they could sit in silence too, without feeling the need to fill the gaps with mindless chatter. That was something rare in such a new relationship, and he seemed to know when to give her space to think. Guilt was nagging at her again, in the now-familiar way it so often did, when she let herself drift too far away from her old life. She hadn't been entirely honest with Elliott when she'd said she wanted to pretend to be someone else, anyone but the widow of Finn Douglas-Jones. What she'd wanted was to pretend that she was Elliott's partner, in business and in life. That was much more specific, and much less faithful to her husband's memory. She couldn't help how she felt, but that didn't mean she had to share it with anyone else. Least of all Elliott.

'So what's so special about the crab at Finbar Bay then? I thought the fish market at Port Kara was good enough to meet the centre's every need.'

'It's supposed to be the best crab in all of Cornwall and there are certain boats which will only sell their catch out of Finbar Bay. We're really lucky to have the fish market on the harbour in Port Kara, but I just wanted to see if Finbar Bay lives up to its promise. It was an excuse to take you out to lunch, too.'

'You don't need an excuse to take me out to lunch.'

'Maybe not an excuse, but just a good reason to make the time. One that wouldn't raise anyone else's suspicions.'

'Do you think I'm being silly about all this cloak and dagger stuff?' Anna watched Elliott as she spoke, and he shook his head.

'No, I get it.' He negotiated a hair pin bend ahead, keeping his eyes firmly fixed on the road. 'Finbar Bay's just over the hill ahead, but you can see the harbour if you look to your right now.'

Anna turned her head and caught a glimpse of the sea between the twin hills, which the road cut a path through the middle. There were boats bobbing in the harbour and she could just see the top of the church spire.

'There are so many beautiful places down here. How did you decide on Port Kara?' It was her turn to question him. If Elliott hadn't told her about his past, she could easily have believed he was Port Kara born-and-bred. He was so at home there, and he seemed to know every inch of the cliff-face and coastal path that led down from the centre to the beach.

'It found me. I looked at lots of places that had the potential to run an adventure centre, I even looked at a place just outside Finbar Bay, but Port Kara just felt right. The cliffs there are dramatic and challenging for climbing, and the surf is perfect. The network of caves that were used for smuggling were also a big selling point, but most of all I just felt at home from the moment I pulled up in my car. Why did you take so many holidays in Port Kara? I'm guessing you must have felt its pull, too?'

'Finn loved the surfing, and I used to paint a lot back then; the seascapes were perfect. But, like you, I just felt at home there. Running the restaurant was stressful and I remember feeling like a weight had been lifted, every time I saw the 'Welcome to Port Kara' signpost when we drove into the village. And, of course, Albie loves it too.'

'Don't you paint anymore?'

'No, I haven't felt like it since I lost Finn. I tried a few times, but I couldn't seem to finish anything. I was planning to do some painting whilst I was down here this time but working at the centre hasn't left me much time.'

'I'm sorry.' Elliott's tone was gentle.

'I'm not. The truth is, I don't know what I would have done with myself if I hadn't had the centre to go to. It's reminded me of my first love, too. Cooking has always been my passion and my escape, but I even lost the motivation to do that after Finn died. I was going through the motions, but I wasn't feeling it. Having to step in at the centre made me throw myself back into it whole-heartedly and I'm the happiest I've been for a long time.'

'Since Finn died?' Elliott turned to look at her as he brought the car to a halt, in a small carpark opposite the harbour in Finbar Bay.

'Yes.' Once again, she wasn't telling him the whole truth. There'd been times in the last year or so of Finn's life when she'd wondered if they were drifting apart. Before that they'd headed to Port Kara whenever they had time off together, but in that last year, if she was really honest with herself, there'd been times when Finn had chosen to spend his free time doing other things. There'd been a couple of trips with Jasper, one to go sky-diving in the Nevada desert, and another trip scuba-diving in Israel. He'd even managed a weekend skiing black runs in Val D'Isere. Anna had stayed at home with Albie, running the restaurant. She'd taken her holidays separately, when Finn was back at the restaurant, flying over to her parents' place in Portugal or going to visit friends. She wasn't lonely, but that wasn't the point.

She couldn't help wondering what would have happened if they'd had children, but she hadn't wanted to give up on them either. They'd both worked long hours to get the business up and running, and, once it became such a big success, she could understand Finn's desire to make the most of the opportunities that had come his way. She'd told herself that they'd work through it and come out the other side, but now she wasn't sure that they ever would have done. It was why she was so happy at the centre — happier than she'd been for at least a year before Finn's death. But she didn't want to admit that to Elliott, or to herself. She'd loved Finn, she really had, but his death had put him on a pedestal and things hadn't been as perfect as she'd wanted to remember them being.

'I checked with the restaurant and they're happy for us to take Albie in, even if it rains,' Elliott said as they got out of the car. 'The sky's looking a bit threatening.'

'I love a good storm, especially the electrical sort where the lightning illuminates the sky. Although maybe not in this dress.'

'Let's get to the restaurant, then.' Elliott got Albie out of the back and they headed along the path that ran parallel with the harbour. Even the air smelt of salt, and the rising wind made the dog unusually skittish.

'I hope Albie calms down a bit by the time we get to the restaurant. He hasn't been like this since he was a baby.' Anna's hand brushed against Elliott's as she drew level with him, whilst he kept a firm hold of Albie's lead with the other hand. Curling her fingers around his, she slipped her hand inside Elliott's. They were taking things slowly, but every time she touched him her body seemed to jolt. At first she'd put it down to guilt, but she had to admit now that it wasn't that. Her body wasn't just reacting to his touch any more, even the *thought* of him touching her made her tingle. She'd forgotten how something as simple as a brush of the hand could make her heart race, so that she could actually feel it beating.

'He'll be fine. I think he's just reacting to the wind.' Elliott laughed as Albie started chasing his tail. 'And if they don't want him in the restaurant, they'll have to do without me too.'

'Thank you.'

'What for?'

'Everything.' She stopped, as he turned to look at her.

'It's me who should be thanking you, I don't know what I'd have done if you hadn't stepped in to help out at the centre.'

'We were obviously meant to find each other then.' Facing him, every fibre in Anna's body was reacting to their proximity. This didn't feel like Jasper said it would, though — a stepping stone to something serious — and she was scared.

'Anna, you're amazing. I just wish — '

'Don't wish for anything else, let's just enjoy this while it lasts.' She was still hiding things from him, still saying the things that she wanted to believe were true; that she would still be able to walk away from this, and him, without her heart suffering another scar. As their lips met, another jolt of electricity passed through her body, and the sky seemed to change colour at that exact moment.

'The storm's broken.' Elliott pulled away from her as another flash of lightning lit up the sky, a low rumble of thunder following in its wake. Within seconds, rain was bouncing off the pavement, and Elliott put his arm around her shoulder. 'Come on — if we run, I can get you to the restaurant before you get soaked to the skin.'

He did his best to protect her as they ran towards the pub on the other side of the harbour. Elliott had told her that The Crab and Winkle pub was owned by the same family that ran the two biggest crabbing boats out of Finbar Bay, and having lunch there would give them a good idea whether the reputation it had for sourcing the best crab in Cornwall was true.

'Are you okay?' Elliott pulled her into the pub doorway and Albie shook himself, showering them both with second-hand rain water.

'There was a bit of me that wasn't wet, but Albie's just taken care of that.' She laughed. 'I probably look like a drowned rat, too.'

'You look great.' His gaze swept over her and she was suddenly aware of the way her damp dress was clinging to her body. 'But are you sure you want to go and eat like this?'

'I'm sure I'll soon dry off. As long as you're sure they won't mind having

Albie in the pub like that. I'm hoping he's already shaken off most of the water that's soaked into his coat.'

'I know James, the guy who runs the pub, and he told me that half the pub is dog friendly, so as long as we stick to the right half, we should be fine.' Elliott smiled. 'And I've still got a pocket full of organic dog treats to keep him quiet. Because I know Albie's body's a temple.'

'More like a dustbin!' It was something else she liked about Elliott — how much he seemed to love Albie and vice versa. Dogs were supposed to be good judges of character and, if that was true, then Elliott was definitely one of the good guys.

* * *

'So, what do you think of the crab?' Elliott put his knife and fork together and pushed his plate away.

'It's amazing. Everything tastes so fresh. I think it would be a great addition to the menu if we can get them to supply the centre.' Anna's dress had finally dried out, but the rain was still battering against the window outside. The view across the harbour would probably have been beautiful if the weather had held out but, as it was, she could barely make out the lamppost on the pavement opposite.

'I was hoping we could take Albie for a walk on the beach this afternoon, but by the look of the weather, we'll be safer holed up here.'

'I'm in no hurry to go anywhere, and neither is Albie by the sounds of him.' Anna laughed as the dog let out another long snore. James had taken him up to the rooms above the pub when they'd first arrived, to give him some lunch of his own and let him dry off. Back downstairs and with a full belly, in the warmth of the pub's family bar, he'd soon curled up for a sleep.

'Why are you in such a hurry to go back to London, then?' Elliott's question had come out of nowhere and she wasn't sure she could come up with an answer. Not one that would make sense to anyone else.

'It's just home.'

'It was.'

'I could ask you why you were so keen to leave.'

'You know the answer to that.'

'What would I even do if I stayed here?'

'I suppose it's too much to hope that you'd want to stay at the centre.' Elliott reached out and touched her hand. 'You'd want more than that, wouldn't you?'

'I think the centre's brilliant, but I'm used to having my own business, and I can't imagine working for someone else long-term.' It was a half-truth. The reality was that she couldn't really imagine working alongside anyone other than Finn, not long-term. It would feel like another scar on his memory.

'I couldn't go back to working for someone else either, but that doesn't mean you've got to go it alone.' Elliott looked like he'd been about to say something else, when James pulled out a chair opposite Anna and sat down.

'So, do you want Finbar Bay Fisheries to supply crab to the adventure centre?' He had a strong Cornish accent and he was straight down to business.

'I think we do, don't we?' Elliott turned towards Anna.

'Yes, it'll make a great addition to the menu.'

'Your wife knows what she's talking about.' James slapped his hand on the table. 'And you won't get better than the crab my brothers bring in. People come from miles around to eat here and it's all down to that.'

'We want to shift to a more local menu. Cornwall has got so much to offer.' Elliott didn't miss a beat this time, and he clearly wasn't going to bother putting James right about them not being married. He was obviously okay with it, and he seemed to understand why she didn't want to tell everyone about Finn. What she couldn't understand was why everyone seemed to assume that she and Elliott were married.

'Who supplies the pork to the centre?' James looked at Anna as he spoke.

'We've got a few suppliers, but I think breakfast is one of the areas where we could change a few things to make a real impact. At the moment it's good, but what we really want is for it to be outstanding.' Anna bit her lip. She'd caught herself saying 'we' more and more often when she talked about the centre. Maybe that was why everyone thought she and Elliott were much more to each other than they really were.

'There's a free-range farmer out at Falstow, who produces pork from rare-breed pigs on two hundred acres of woodland. You'll never have tasted bacon or sausages like it.' James grinned. 'It'll revolutionise your breakfasts.'

'That sounds amazing. Do you think we could squeeze in one more supplier visit tomorrow?' Anna looked at Elliott.

Spending time with him hadn't just reignited her passion for sourcing the very best ingredients possible, she was having more fun than she could remember having for such a long time. Even getting soaked to the skin had been fun with him, and the only downside was how fast the time was going. If they could fit in another supplier visit on the second day, it would give them an excuse to spend a bit more time together. No one would wonder why they'd spent so much time together away from the centre, if they could report back on how many new suppliers they'd secured. It was one thing using the trip as an explanation for Billy and the others, but she still needed to justify it to herself, too. If she admitted just how much she liked being with Elliott, the guilt might overwhelm her completely.

'I wish we had the time to make it a whole week.' He gave her such an intense look that she flushed, all too aware that James was sitting just across the table from them.

'I wish I'd had this sort of support from my wife when we were together.' His Cornish accent made the statement sound sing-song, even as he frowned. 'She hated it when I was fishing and moaned like billy-o about all the time I spent on the boats with my brothers. Then I set this place up and she moaned that I was always in the bar, talking to customers. I couldn't do right for doing wrong, but the truth was she didn't get it. She didn't understand why the crabbing was so important to us and why I wanted to be part of that, either on the boats, or selling the end product in the pub. She ran off with a double glazing salesman in the end, and I think she got the quiet life she always wanted. Not to mention the Victorian-style conservatory she'd been harping on about for years!'

'Sorry.' Anna had to fight the urge to laugh, but James and Elliott were smiling too.

'It's alright; she got her conservatory

and I got the pub. We both got the lives we wanted in the end. I can't abide even looking at the bloody things now, though. My brother suggested we put on a conservatory out the back of the pub, for extra dining space and to give the customers a great view of the bay, but I'm not ready for that yet.' James grinned again. 'Still, you two seem to have it all. Let me go and get the number for the pig farm and you can give Barney a call, then we can talk terms on the crab.'

James got up and headed off through a door on the other side of the bar.

'Who'd have thought a conservatory could end a marriage?' Elliott smiled, his dark brown eyes filled with that same warmth that had made her feel safe from the first time she'd seen him, when he'd promised her everything would be okay. Whoever he ended up marrying would be a lucky woman, and she couldn't help wondering what it would be like to have someone like Elliott to lean on and know you could always trust to put you first. The trouble was there wasn't someone like Elliott, there was just him, and she wasn't going to be the lucky one.

'I've really enjoyed today.' Anna let her fingers graze his, as she reached out for her glass, that familiar bolt of electricity shooting through her body as she did.

'It's not over yet, we've still got tonight. And tomorrow.' Anna nodded, unable to answer him as a lump formed in her throat. Tomorrow wasn't promised, she knew that as well as anyone. And, even if it came, it suddenly sounded far too short. Time didn't stop for anyone, and it wouldn't stop for her and Elliott, no matter how much she might want it to.

★   ★   ★

'I didn't think the rain was ever going to stop.' Anna had linked her arm through Elliott's as they walked along the path that ran alongside the river on the edge of Finbar Bay. The river fed into the estuary that led straight out to sea and was flanked on both sides by lush greenery, which looked almost tropical after the heavy rainfall. The trees were actually steaming now that the sun was out and Albie was wetter than ever from investigating the undergrowth, to see whether an unsuspecting rabbit might be hiding out in there from the aftermath of the storm.

'This is something else I love about living here. Most of the time the weather is brilliant and I can spend as much time outdoors as I like, but when the weather turns, it tends to be pretty dramatic.' Elliott shrugged, knowing that Anna understood, even if she kept insisting that London was where her heart was. She'd been so enthralled by everywhere they'd visited, and so fired up by the idea of running somewhere like the farm shop at Polton Dairy Farm, that he was sure she understood the pull of Cornwall. If anywhere could weave its magic and make her change her mind about leaving, it would be Port Kara, or Cornwall itself. It wouldn't be Elliott; it *couldn't* be Elliott.

Much as he might want to, he couldn't promise her what she needed to hear to have any chance of convincing her to stay. He couldn't promise to take the safe path, or give up the life he loved, which was what he'd need to do to stop Anna worrying every time he walked out the door. He'd spent years living up to someone else's expectations and he'd been miserable the whole time. Even if Anna wanted him to make those promises to her, he knew he couldn't keep them. It would be a strange kind of torture having her stay, but not be with him. Eventually, whatever it was they had together would have to come to an end and, if she stayed in Port Kara, the chances were that she'd find her Mr Steady, and Elliott would have to stand by and watch. But even that seemed preferable to her leaving altogether in less than a month. Either way it was going to hurt him, he'd accepted that now, but friendship seemed better than nothing at all. They'd promised each other to live in the moment, though, for as long as the summer lasted, so he pushed thoughts of what might happen next to the back of his mind. 'Albie seems to be having the time of his life.'

'He is, bless him.' Anna grinned, making her bluey-green eyes sparkle in the way that always floored him. 'The poor thing's got no clue that, even if he does manage to flush out a rabbit, he'll never catch it whilst he's on this wander lead.'

No sooner had she spoken than something rustled in the bushes just up ahead of them. A black ball of fur shot out of the undergrowth and Albie surged forward as far as his wander lead would let him go, pulling Anna and Elliott forward in the process. As Albie almost reached the black blur that was now his prey, it shot to the left, landing in the river with a loud splash. Throwing Albie's lead at Elliott before he even had a chance to react, Anna ran forward, and seconds later there was an even louder splash. She was in the water, too.

'What the hell are you doing? Are you okay?' Elliott ran to the edge of the riverbank, still keeping a firm hold of Albie, who looked like he might join Anna in the water at any moment. The water was running fast, but Anna had already managed to get to the edge, with the ball of black fluff under her arm.

'It disappeared under the water and I didn't want it to drown. I think it's a dog.' Anna's hair was plastered to the side of her head but, even covered in green algae, she managed to look more like a mermaid than a drowned rat.

'It could have been a badger for all you knew.' Elliott quickly tied Albie's lead to a tree on the edge of the bank, and reached out his arms towards Anna.

'It doesn't matter, I still didn't want it to drown.'

'It would probably have sunk its teeth into you if it had been, rather than shown you any thanks for saving it.' He didn't want to admit that he'd probably have jumped in, if Anna hadn't been so quick, even it had just been a rabbit. His heart had been in his mouth for the couple of seconds when he hadn't been able to see her in the fast-flowing river. If something had happened to her . . . he couldn't even bear to think about it. 'You could have drowned.'

'I'm fine. I think adrenaline just took over.' She fell against him as he pulled her and the little dog clear of the water. 'I don't think this little chap would have lasted long. He feels like a bag of bones.'

'Let's take a look at him.' Elliott lifted the dog out of her arms. She was right, there was nothing to him, and there were bald patches obvious even in the wet coat that clung to his tiny body. 'He looks like a stray to me; he's not wearing a collar.'

'What are we going to do with him?

We can't just leave him here. He might be hurt too.'

'If you're sure you're okay, we can go back into Finbar Bay and ask James whether there's a vet who can check if it's microchipped.' Elliott turned the little dog over in his arms. 'He's a she, by the way!'

'Oh, poor little girl.' Anna nodded her head. 'I'm fine, I just want to get her checked over.'

'We can ask James to ring the local council and see if anyone has reported their dog missing, then share her picture on the centre's social media pages once she's dry and a bit more recognisable to whoever might have lost her.'

'And what if no-one comes forward to claim her?' Anna looked like she might burst into tears at the thought.

'We'll cross that bridge when we come to it.' Holding the shivering dog closer to him to try and warm her up, Elliott could feel her little heart thudding under his hand. She didn't look well cared for and, if he'd been a betting man, he'd have gambled a big stake that no-one would come forward to claim her. But, if they didn't, he'd already made up his mind he was going to keep her. She'd landed in their lives unexpectedly, in much the same way that Anna had landed in his. He had no choice but to let Anna go when she was ready, but he could keep the little dog they'd found together, and maybe that would be enough to get him through. He'd seen a new side to Anna, though. She'd been fearless when it came to jumping into the river to save that dog. That made her ten times braver than his clients, who took part in engineered adrenaline highs, that were carefully monitored and controlled by well-qualified guides. There was a tiny bit of him that couldn't help holding on to the hope that maybe she'd learn to embrace adventure and make a life in Port Kara after all. Except hope could end up being far more dangerous than any adrenaline high, if you let it.

8

Albie raced across the sand and Anna held her breath, hoping that her new-found trust in him wouldn't be misplaced and that he'd come back when she called. Leaping on to the tennis ball he was chasing, he skidded to a halt, sending up a shower of sand.

'Come on Albie, come on Splash; back you come.' Albie turned and looked at her, before galloping back in her direction, the little black dog that she'd rescued from the river in Finbar Bay following hot on his heels.

'My dog seems to be a good influence on yours,' Elliott laughed. 'He actually seems to prefer chasing around with her now, rather than mugging holidaymakers for their picnics.'

'I know, but I still think he might let me down every time I risk it. Especially after he leapt into the sea after you that day.'

223

'He's not the only one capable of leaping into the water unexpectedly.' Elliott caught hold of her hand and pulled her towards him, so that they were standing face to face. 'But I'm glad you did. I couldn't imagine life without Splash now.'

'I guess I'm just lucky that didn't end up being my nickname, seeing as I made a much bigger splash than she did when I hit the water.' She shivered, as he pushed a strand of hair behind her ear.

'That's not the first thing that springs to mind when I think about you.'

'I'm glad you decided to adopt Splash when no one came forward to claim her; she deserved a second chance and I can't think of anyone better to give it to her than you.'

'Everyone deserves a second chance.' He had that intense look in his eyes again, that he seemed to get so often just lately. They hadn't talked about where their relationship might be going since they'd had that first conversation about keeping things casual. Nothing

224

about it felt casual to her anymore, but the tick-tock of the time slipping away until her lease of the cottage was over was getting almost deafening. Leaning towards him, she tried to drown out the nagging voice in her head, as he lowered his head towards her. Breathing in the scent of his sandalwood after-shave, mingled in with the sea air, she wanted to freeze the moment. It would be so simple if there was no before or after to cloud her thoughts, and when they were kissing it was the one time she couldn't think about anything else but Elliott. The spell was always broken eventually, though. This time the sound of a seagull screeching overhead made her pull away and look up. It was impossible to freeze the perfect moment: one way or another, the real world always found a way of crashing in.

'Have you got time to come to mine for a drink?' Anna clipped on Albie's lead when they were about a hundred yards away from the cottage; she didn't want to risk him running off at the last minute, which he might well do if he realised their walk with Splash and Albie was nearly over.

'I can always make time.' She knew Elliott was due back at the centre for the welcome dinner with a new group of guests. She was gradually trying to pull back from running the restaurant, doing less shifts and leaving Billy to supervise the agency staff on his own for more of the time.

Elliott followed her up the path to the front door of the cottage, and she handed him Albie's lead as she unlocked the door. It had almost become a routine since he'd decided to keep Splash, the two of them meeting to walk the dogs on the beach every day once the tourists had started to pack up and empty the carpark, leaving the mile and a half long stretch of sand that was Port Kara's main beach almost deserted. She loved that time of day better than any other and it was something else she'd miss when she got back to London. Considering that Albie had nearly been responsible for Splash drowning, the two dogs were now best of friends, and he'd definitely miss her too. It was funny how quickly somewhere could come to feel like home, and Myrtle Cottage was the closest thing they'd had to that since selling the restaurant. She and Finn had lived in the flat above the restaurant with Albie, but when she'd sold the business, she'd taken out a rental lease on a furnished flat, putting most of their stuff into storage until she decided where to put down proper roots. There was a two-bedroomed terraced cottage she'd seen in Highgate, with an astronomical rent and a little garden that might cheer Albie up a bit when he was missing the beach. She'd seen it online, and it had reminded her of Myrtle Cottage just enough for her to email the agent and offer a rental deposit without even seeing the place. It wouldn't be the same, but they'd moved on before and survived, so they could do it again. She'd already given notice on the other flat, so they should be moved in by October, and someone else would be enjoying the view from Myrtle Cottage out over Port Kara beach by then.

'I bet you never thought this would be your life, did you?' Anna laughed, as she brought the coffees back into the sitting room. Splash was laid out across Elliott's legs, and Albie was lying on his feet. He couldn't have moved if he wanted to and Anna wondered if the dogs had picked up on something, wanting to keep him there as much as she did. But his duty to the centre would be calling soon and he'd leave, no matter how hard Albie and Splash tried to keep him there. It was like a siren's call to the sailors of old and Anna was just as powerless to stop it.

'I have to say I didn't. I've never even thought about getting a dog before, but I'd already fallen for Albie, so when Splash turned up it seemed like it was meant to be.' Elliott shrugged. 'I'd never have had a dog when I was working such long hours in London, it wouldn't have been fair, and I never had any pets as a kid because dad hates them.'

'How can anyone hate dogs?' Anna set the cups down on the coffee table and sat next to Elliott on the sofa.

'He hates anything that doesn't have a purpose in his eyes, and for him that's anything that costs money rather than makes it.'

'What about your mum?'

'She's got three cats now. And a tattoo.' Elliott laughed. 'Dad hated cats even more than dogs and he told her if she ever got a tattoo he'd divorce her. So the first thing she did when they finally split up was go out and get a tattoo, and within three weeks she'd bought three kittens from the same litter, too.'

'Does she regret it now?'

'Getting the kittens or the tattoo?'

'No.' Anna shook her head, wondering if the question she was about to ask was too personal. 'I meant does she regret staying in the marriage for so long.'

'I should think so and I wish she

hadn't. I wish I'd stood up to him when I was younger too and had the guts to tell him I didn't want to be a carbon copy of him.'

'But then you wouldn't have ended up here, or been the person you are.'

'Maybe.'

'I'm glad you're here and I'm glad you're the person you are.' As Anna reached out for his hand, Splash jumped off his lap.

'I'm glad you're here too.' He took her face in his hands as he spoke and she tried not to think about the reason she was in Port Kara, or what Finn would say if he knew how deep her feelings for Elliott had become. But then she realised she couldn't imagine it even if she'd wanted to, because she couldn't remember what her husband's voice had sounded like anymore. There was no hiding from it. Elliott was pushing him out, and she had to do something about it before it was too late.

* * *

The hammering on the door of Elliott's flat was so frantic, he'd half expected to be able to smell smoke when he opened it. Instead, it was Anna standing there, her face as white as the surf that turned over with the incoming tide on Port Kara beach.

'Are you okay? You look terrible.' Elliott stood back as she charged into the flat, Albie right behind her and a black laptop bag clutched to her chest.

'I feel terrible. I've lost everything and I can't even remember what he sounds like.' Anna took a shuddering breath, her voice cracking on the words.

'Do you mean Finn?' Elliott already knew the answer to the question, even before she nodded. But she wasn't making any sense and he needed her to slow down if he was going to try and help her.

'Yes. I realised tonight, after you left, that I was forgetting things about him. I tried to imagine talking to him again, like I used to when he first died, but I couldn't even remember what his voice sounded like.' Her face was wet with tears now and her voice was still coming out in a rush.

'You're probably just panicking that you can't.' It was hard to know what to say without making things worse. He knew how badly losing Finn had affected her, but he'd never seen her grief this naked before and it twisted something deep in his gut. How could he help her, when all she really wanted was Finn?

'I'm not imagining it; I really can't remember what it sounded like. I wanted to watch one of the videos I had of him on the laptop, just so I could hear him again. But the files are all corrupted and it's all gone.' The last word turned into a sob and Albie was pacing up and down, not knowing how to comfort Anna any more than Elliott did. At least he could try something practical.

'Can I take a look?'

'You can, but there's an error message coming up that looks like a no entry sign every time I try to open one of the files.'

'Let me get you a drink and you can sit down and try to relax, whilst I see if I can work out what's wrong.'

'I don't want a drink.' Anna was shaking her head, as if to emphasise the point. 'Please just have a look at it and see if there's anything you can do.'

'There must be other copies of some of the videos; did you upload some of them to social media sites?'

'A few, and there'll be some that other people might have kept a copy of. But I'm the only one with copies of lots of them. When I changed my phone after Finn died, I just uploaded the video files from the phone on to my laptop. It was so stupid, I should have made copies straight away.'

'Don't worry, it'll be okay,' Elliott just hoped he wouldn't turn out to be lying. He'd rather have a cliff-face to scale down any day; this had far higher stakes.

'Any luck yet?' Anna barely gave him

sixty seconds before she started asking the question, leaning over his shoulder and fidgeting from foot to foot.

'Just give me a minute.' He held his breath as he waited for the computer to load a webpage, and the log-in name automatically loaded. 'Do you know the password you used for the storage cloud?'

'I think it's Albie123, with a capital A.' Anna was still looking over his shoulder, as he entered the details.

'Is this one of the videos?' He clicked on a MP4 video file and an image of Finn running towards the sea, with a surfboard under his arm and Albie at his feet, filled the screen. Elliott watched the video with a weird mixture of massive relief at having located a back-up copy of the files, and a twinge of irrational jealousy. It was crazy to be jealous of Albie chasing after Finn, but it was another reminder that Anna had shared a life with another man. A man she'd still be devoted to, if he'd lived. He hated himself for it, but the feeling was just as much beyond his control as Anna's decision to leave would be.

'Thank you.' She leant over the back of the chair, and kissed his cheek. It was just a brief brush of the lips and she took the laptop off him in a single move. The sound of Finn's laughter filled the space between them and, when he turned to look at her, she was staring at the screen as if there was nothing else in the world.

'Do you want that drink now?'

'Uh huh.' She didn't look up at him, as she sank into one of the other armchairs, loading another video of Finn.

'What can I get you? A coffee, or a glass of wine?'

'Whatever you're having; I don't care.' She meant the drink, he knew she did, but he couldn't help thinking that the statement was loaded with so much more. All she'd wanted was to hear Finn's voice again and he realised, like a punch to the gut, that she'd never care that much about him. He was just a way to spend the summer, someone to pass the time with. She'd already met the love of her life and he'd been too late. As much as he wanted to tell himself that it didn't matter, and that he'd never set out to have that sort of relationship with her, there was a hollow feeling in his chest that hadn't been there before.

9

Billy's singing wasn't nearly as good as his cooking, but that didn't stop him belting out every song that came on to the radio. Anna had to press her lips together to stop herself laughing as he tried to hit the high note in a Sia song that the local DJ had described as her biggest hit.

'Have you ever had singing lessons?' She looked at Billy as she took a punnet of raspberries out of the fridge and he shook his head. 'Well, maybe you should think about it!'

'Cheeky!' Billy grinned, and responded by belting out the final chorus with even more enthusiasm.

'Thank goodness for that. A bit of respite at last.' Anna let out a low whistle, as the DJ announced that the news was up next.

'The headlines at four on Three Ports

Radio.' The newsreader had a more serious tone than the DJ, but the big local news was never anything very troubling. 'The international surfing festival at Port Tremellien, has been hit by a tragedy with the death of an un-named surfer.'

'Oh no, please not again.' Anna dropped the punnet of raspberries, sending them scattering across the kitchen workstation. Her neck prickled as the newsreader carried on the report, and Billy seemed to freeze on the spot.

'Eyewitnesses say that the surfer was leading a group and was knocked unconscious when two of the competitors collided. Attempts to resuscitate the man, who is said to be a local resident in his mid-thirties, were unsuccessful and paramedics pronounced him dead at the scene. Police say the man will not be named until his next of kin have been informed.'

'It won't be Elliott, Anna. There are hundreds of people at the festival, and Elliott's too good at what he does to be caught up in something like that.'

'Finn was good at what he did too.' She couldn't stop shivering and, as she looked at Billy, he seemed to be going in and out of focus. She had a horrible feeling she might be about to pass out.

'I'll get you a chair, I think you need to sit down.' Billy ran out to the restaurant and came back with one of the dining chairs twenty seconds later.

'I'm okay.'

'No you're not. Sit down before you fall down.' Billy more or less forced her into the chair, even as she continued shaking her head.

'This can't be happening again.'

'It isn't. I know Elliott and the rest of the team who've gone down to Port Tremellien today. They're all professionals, they do this stuff for a living, they know the risks and they know how to avoid them.'

'But what if it is him? Can you try ringing?' Poor Billy; he looked almost as bad as she felt. He probably had no idea what to do with a hysterical woman, and he looked almost relieved to have the excuse to go off and make the call.

'I'll go and use the phone in the restaurant and see whether any of the bar staff have heard something from one of the guides.'

'Okay.' Anna couldn't stay sitting down. The waiting was worse than anything and the DJ had put a feel-good summer song on straight after the news report. Yanking the lead out of the radio, she started to put the raspberries back into the punnet. Half of them were already too damaged to use, crushed by their fall on to the hard surface, just like Finn had been. Was Elliott lying somewhere now, cold and lifeless? She couldn't go through it again.

'I left a message for him, but there haven't been any calls into the centre. I'm sure if something bad had happened we'd have heard by now.' Billy's words were obviously intended to be reassuring, as he came back into the kitchen, but the look on his face told another story. He was worried too.

'I hope you're right, but I can't think straight. Can you manage the rest of the prep, if I go up to the flat and check on the dogs? I think I'll be more of a hindrance than a help to you otherwise.' Anna turned to the young sous chef and he nodded.

'No problem, we've already done most of the prep anyway. If a call comes through to the bar to confirm that Elliott and the others are okay, I'll come up and find you.'

'Thanks.' Anna touched his shoulder as she moved past him, hoping that he couldn't feel her shaking.

As she opened the door of the flat less than a minute later, Albie lifted his head off the dog sofa to acknowledge her presence, and then stretched out again, making the most of the fact that Splash wasn't taking up the space beside him. The little black dog was pawing at the full-length windows which looked out over the beach, and she started to whine as soon as she spotted Anna.

'You know, don't you?' She bent down and scooped up the dog. Maybe she was reading too much into it, but weren't animals supposed to have a sixth sense about this sort of thing? Albie always seemed to pick up on when she was upset, but this time he seemed more interested in making the most of the sunny spot by the window.

Sitting down on the sofa with Splash still in her arms, she checked her phone. She'd texted Elliott on the way up to the flat to tell him to ring her as soon as he got the message. She must have checked for a reply at least a hundred times over the next half an hour, and she felt like hurling her phone out of the window and over the cliff when there was still no response.

'Anna.' Elliott was suddenly standing in the doorway of the flat, his dark eyes much more serious than normal.

'I thought you were dead!' Splash jumped off her lap before she could even stand up, and hurtled towards Elliott like a bullet out of a gun.

'I'm sorry. I tried to call, but it was chaos at Port Tremellien with everything that happened, and then I couldn't get a signal.'

'Are you okay? Is everyone else okay?' She walked towards him, her legs shaking, terrified that she might just have conjured him up and he wouldn't really be there.

'No one from the centre was involved in the accident, we weren't even in the water at the time it happened. The group we were leading were all in the amateur round, but it was a group of professionals trying to qualify for a place in the World Series who had the accident. We were just watching and thinking how amazing they were, and suddenly all hell broke loose.'

'Did you actually see the accident?'

'We tried to help out with first aid when they brought him onto the beach, but there was nothing anyone could do.'

'That's so sad.'

'I'm sorry I scared you again.'

'I can't keep doing this, Elliott.' Anna turned away from him. If she looked at his face, she wouldn't be able to say what she had to say. 'I promised myself I wouldn't get involved with anyone who got their kicks from putting their life on the line again, but all you've done since I met you is take risks. Rescuing that guy from the sea at Jasper's beach party was bad enough, but then I have to hear on the radio that there's been another surfing accident when you're there. It wasn't you this time, but it easily could have been. And it might be next time.'

'I was never in any danger rescuing that guy from the beach. Like I said at the time, he was just an idiot who'd drunk too much and got himself into trouble because he didn't take advice. I'm always careful and follow all the safety procedures. Nothing bad is *ever* going to happen to me; it's not going to happen to you again.' Elliott echoed Billy's words as he moved to stand behind her, and she had to fight the urge to turn around and let him put his arms around her. It would have been so easy to let him comfort her, to feel the strength of his body against hers. Nothing could happen to someone like him — except it could — and lying to herself wasn't going to work anymore. She cared about him. A lot. But she couldn't lose someone she loved again. It was too late to stop herself from falling in love with him, as hard as she'd tried, but she could control when it ended if she walked away now.

'You can't make me that promise — no one can.'

'I could stop doing all the things I love and get hit by a car, or fall down and hit my head walking Splash, or get ill completely out of the blue. None of us can make the promise to always be there for someone else, Anna, even if we want that more than anything else.' He took hold of her shoulders and turned her to face him, even as she tried to resist. 'But we said we'd make the most of whatever time we have together and that's all anyone can really promise. It was only supposed to be the summer, but I've got to tell you this: I don't think that's going to be enough for me. I want you to stay and I promise you I will be here for you as long as I can. Seeing what happened on the beach today made me realise something — I love you.'

'I love you, too.' Tears were streaming down her face and Splash was whining again. Even Albie had got up from his spot in the sun to see what was going on.

'So we've got to make this work, right?' Elliott's voice was gentle and she found herself nodding, even though she knew it could never work. The guilt of falling in love again had almost crippled her, but it was hearing about the accident on the radio that had shattered her last bit of hope into a million pieces. She could never stay with Elliott, not if she wanted to survive. But he'd said he wanted to live in the moment and right now the only place she wanted to be was in his arms. If she stayed, he'd feel suffocated, and she'd be terrified every time he went to work. Somehow she'd find the courage to tell him that she was going and make him understand that it was the best for both of them. But, until then, she was determined to make every moment count.

* * *

Anna couldn't move. She was trying to run towards the sea, but her legs wouldn't cooperate. Elliott had broken his promise; it was happening again, he was in the water and she was the only one who could save him.

'No!' Anna jolted awake as her body jerked in response to the nightmare. It felt so real, it took her a moment or two to realise where she was. In bed, in Myrtle Cottage, and Elliott was safe. But for how long?

Getting into the shower, she let the hot water run, not wanting to face the day. She had to leave, it was so clear now, and even though that had been her plan all along, it suddenly seemed gut-wrenching. Not getting to see Elliott every day would be torture, but still not as bad as living every second when he was out on some adrenaline adventure or another, waiting for that call. He was at far more risk than Finn had ever been, because he put other people before his own safety. Finn had only ever had himself to look out for, and it had still ended badly.

At least she'd be leaving the kitchen at the centre in good hands. Billy had really risen to the challenge and his college had agreed he could finish his qualification by work-based learning, so he'd be able to head up the catering team most of the time. They'd found a couple of agency staff who worked well, and she hoped at least one of them would be willing to take on a permanent position. The last thing she wanted to do was leave Elliott in the lurch.

She got dressed almost robotically; it was like she was closing off her feelings already. How many more mornings would she get up and look at the view across the beach from Myrtle Cottage to the headland where the centre was? Less than she could count on one hand if either of the agency staff agreed to step in. The centre was Elliott's responsibility, but she wanted to be the one to make the call. Letting him know what she was doing would give him a chance to find a reason why she couldn't possibly go, and every time she looked at him her resolve weakened. She had to make it a *fait accompli* — it was the only way.

Ten minutes later, it was done. She'd offered the job of assistant head chef to one of the agency staff, who'd happily accepted, and had arranged for some additional cover from the agency to start the next day. There was no going back now, no matter how Elliott looked at her with those gorgeous brown eyes of his, or the way she felt when he held her in his arms. It was over, just as she'd known it always would be. Only, back then, she'd had no idea how much it would hurt.

★ ★ ★

Elliott had woken up with the same uneasy feeling in his chest that he'd had when he'd witnessed Anna's reaction to losing the videos of Finn. It was a sort of hollow feeling he couldn't explain, like something essential to his happiness had disappeared. But Anna was still in the centre's kitchen when he'd walked in on Sunday morning, just as he'd expected her to be, making the final breakfasts for the guests about to check out. He enjoyed watching her work, especially when she didn't know he was there. Tucking a strand of hair that had escaped from her ponytail behind her ear, she took a tray of fresh Danish pastries out of the oven and set them down on the stainless-steel surface, before turning and catching sight of him. When she smiled, it still took his breath away. He had to persuade her to stay, no matter what it cost.

'You shouldn't sneak up on a woman when she's carrying a burning hot tray.'

'It's a risk I'm willing to take.' He wanted to pull her into his arms and kiss her, but Billy was only a few feet away, cooking up a storm of bacon and eggs. They hadn't kept their relationship a complete secret from the other staff at the centre, but they'd played it down and public displays of affection were definitely not on the agenda.

'What are you doing this afternoon?' Anna started putting the pastries on to a cooling tray as she spoke.

'Hoping you might be free?' They'd got into the habit of spending every Sunday afternoon and evening together, as it was the only time they were completely free of commitments at the centre.

'I thought we could have a picnic on the cliffs above Dagger's Head? The forecast looks good and I want to make the most of the last days of summer

251

before we have to give in and admit that autumn is here.'

'Me too.' The hollow feeling in his chest intensified. It was already September and he knew her lease only ran for a little bit longer. But he still had time to change her mind and he was banking on it. She wasn't the only one who wanted to put the last days of summer to good use. 'I'll be in the office doing some paperwork; come and find me when you're ready.'

'Okay.' Anna turned back to what she was doing and he tried to look forward to the afternoon he was going to spend with her, but he just couldn't shake the feeling of dread that seemed to have taken up permanent residence in his chest.

The pile of paperwork in his office was something he hated doing at the best of times, but it was doubly difficult when all his mind seemed determined to focus on was ways to persuade Anna to stay. He was looking at a row of figures for the fourth time, trying to take them in, when his mobile rang.

'Hello, Dorton Adventure Centre.'

'Is that Elliott Dorton?' It was a woman's voice, but he didn't recognise it.

'Speaking.'

'Ah, great. It's Janice Sawyer here from the Al Catering Agency.'

'Hi, Janice. Good to hear from you. Hopefully you've had the feedback from my head chef that she's been really pleased with the staff you sent most recently.'

'Yes, and we're really pleased to hear that you're taking Gavin on as assistant head chef. In fact, that's why I'm calling, to confirm you're aware of the finders' fee payable to the agency?'

'Sorry, I'm not with you. Who told you that we're taking Gavin on in a permanent role?' Even as he asked the question, Elliott knew the answer. It was Anna and she'd made her escape plan without even talking to him first.

'Your head chef, Anna Turner. I thought you were aware of the decision?' Janice suddenly sounded flustered and it wasn't her fault that she'd just given him the worst possible news. There'd be no changing Anna's mind — it was already too late.

'I leave those kind of decisions to her, but I'm sure she was planning to tell me when we meet later.' Elliott didn't even know if that was true. Had she been planning to tell him? Or would she just have disappeared without saying anything. 'When's he due to start?'

'Tomorrow, as I understand it. Anna also asked for some additional temporary staffing.'

'Right, that's fine, I'm sure Anna knows what she's doing.'

'And the finders' fee?'

'Of course. How much do we owe you?'

'It's five percent of the first year's salary.' Janice paused. 'So by my calculations, I make that two thousand five hundred pounds.'

'Just email an invoice over and I'll get it sorted. Goodbye.'

'Goodbye, Elliott, and thank you.' Just as the call ended, someone knocked on the door to the office and he looked up, desperately trying to hold it together.

'Come in.'

'Sorry, the breakfast service ran a bit long this morning and I wanted to get everything ready for the picnic.' Anna came into the office, carrying a wicker basket and looking like she didn't have a care in the world. Was it really going to be that easy for her to walk away from the centre, and from him?

'I've just had a call from the Al Catering Agency.'

'Oh.' She set the picnic down on the desk with a thud and stared at him, wordlessly. There was nothing she could say to make it better, and at least she seemed to realise that.

'When were you going to tell me you were leaving?'

'After the picnic. I just wanted us to have one last afternoon together.'

'Were you really going to tell me, or were you just going to leave?' He watched her as he spoke, an unreadable expression crossing her face. 'You weren't, were you? You were just going to go without even telling me.'

'I don't know.' She turned away and looked out of the window, her back towards him. 'What does it matter, anyway? We both knew I was going to go in the end. So when I went, and whether I gave you any warning of that or not, hardly matters, does it?'

'It matters to me. I thought this . . . whatever it is that's been going on between us, meant *something* to you. Even if it was just for the summer. It meant something to me.'

'You were just the stepping stone. That's what Jasper told me.' She turned back to face him, her face blank. 'He said I needed to dip my toe back into the water and date the stepping stone guy, before I'd be ready to meet someone who I could really move on with, after what happened to Finn.'

'Right.'

'I'm sorry, I didn't mean to hurt you.

I thought you knew where we stood and I told you it was never going to be anything serious.'

'I thought I did, too, but I hadn't realised it was quite this clinical. That I was part of some kind of experiment, which was the brainchild of Jasper Holland of all people.'

'This isn't Jasper's fault. He was right, I was stuck, and I'd probably have stayed that way if it hadn't been for you, and I'll always be glad I met you. Let's just remember the summer we had and move on. Like we always planned.'

'So, when do you leave?' Elliott sat on the edge of his desk, and she ran a hand through her hair.

'Tomorrow morning.' She shrugged. 'Now that I've decided to go, I can't see the point in hanging around.'

'Have you told Billy?' If Elliott was the last to know, that would have been the ultimate betrayal, but she shook her head slowly. 'I wanted to wait until tomorrow, to make this afternoon and tonight all about us.'

'I think we both know that's not going to happen, don't we?' He stood up and moved back around to the other side of his desk. 'I've got a mountain of paperwork to get through and you must have packing to do.'

'Elliott, I — '

'There's nothing else you can say, really, is there? Just leave your keys with Billy in the morning.'

'I didn't want it to end like this.' She took a step towards him and he shook his head.

'You wanted it to end, though, didn't you? Like you said, where and when hardly matters now.' He dropped his gaze back down to the paperwork in front of him. 'Goodbye, Anna.'

'Bye, Elliott,' She pulled the office door shut behind her, and Elliott's head dropped into his hands. He hadn't been prepared for this, even though he'd known there was a good chance of it coming. It could never have worked between them, he knew that. But no matter how many times he played that mantra over in his head, he couldn't really make himself believe it.

10

Anna's eyes stung and, when she looked in the mirror, the person staring back at her was someone who'd have no need for a mask on Halloween. Her eyes were bloodshot from crying for most of the night, and the dark circles beneath them underlined the fact that she'd barely slept.

It had seemed like a good idea to keep the fact that she was planning to leave a secret from Elliott until the last minute, but the look on his face had been one of pure contempt. It was like he hated her, and the speed with which he'd got her out of his office had literally taken her breath away. She knew she'd said things he didn't want to hear, things that weren't even true. Jasper had been an idiot if he'd thought Elliott could ever be just a stepping stone. She'd fallen for him harder and faster than she'd ever have believed was possible. But if making Elliott believe that being a gap-filler was all he'd ever been to her meant that he would let her go without a fight, then that's what she needed to do.

She might have spent the night crying over Elliott, and she'd probably do that for a long time to come, but at least she wouldn't have to spend the rest of her life wondering when he'd be snatched away from her. Controlling when and how it ended was all she had left once she'd realised she was in love with him.

The suitcases stacked up in the corner of the room looked so insignificant compared with what they represented. It wasn't even two months since she'd arrived at Myrtle Cottage but it had been life changing, and now she was moving on again, and even Albie looked fed up at the prospect.

'Do you want some breakfast, boy?' Filling his bowl with food, she set it down on the kitchen floor and walked away.

'Please don't tell me you hate me, too?' Anna nudged the bowl towards him with her foot, but he just gave it a half-hearted sniff and turned his back on her again. 'How about a walk? We can go up and say goodbye to Billy and give our legs a good stretch before the long drive home.'

It was crazy, talking to a dog as if he actually understood her, but when Albie spotted her unhooking the lead from the back of the kitchen door, he showed the first sign of anything approaching interest that he'd demonstrated all morning.

Clipping his lead on, they headed out down the path from Myrtle Cottage to the beach for what would probably be the last time. There was no way she was letting him run free today of all days, though. She didn't want to give him the chance to run off. Not when she'd promised herself that they'd be on the road by eleven at the latest to beat the high tide that would cut off the cottage for hours after that. They might even be back in London by dinner time that way. She couldn't pick up the keys to the cottage in Highgate until the middle of September, but at least there'd be no chance of running into Elliott when they were nearly three hundred miles apart. She knew she wouldn't run into him on the beach either. It was Monday morning and he'd be welcoming in a new group of guests. He'd throw himself into work, the way he always did, and his real love: life as a risk-taking adrenaline junkie. He might think he'd miss her, and she had no doubt he'd been hurt by the way she'd ended things, but he'd move on, much sooner than she would, and she was happy for him. Maybe he'd even find a woman who loved nothing better than leaping off the side of a cliff, hanging on to a bit of rope that barely looked any thicker than Albie's lead. The thought of that other woman sitting in his apartment and lying in his arms was almost unbearable, and a fresh crop of tears sprung up in her eyes as she carried on across the sand.

Why couldn't she have fallen in love with someone safe this time around, boring even? And why couldn't Jasper have been right about Elliott being the perfect stepping stone, instead of everything she wasn't looking for and everything she wanted, all rolled into one?

Suddenly Albie was barking furiously and almost pulling her arm out of the socket in his determination to move forward. Looking up, she saw an unmistakeable ball of black fur hurtling towards her; the same ball of fur who'd made her jump into the river in Finbar Bay. It was Splash and she was all by herself.

'Come here, girl.' Anna tried to grab hold of the little dog, as Splash and Albie greeted each other with so much enthusiasm they almost knocked her flying.

'Whatever you do, don't let her go!' A man's voice called out and, when Anna looked up, Jasper was sprinting across the sand towards them. Hooking her hand into the dog's collar, she did as he asked.

'Thank goodness you got her.' For such a fitness fanatic, Jasper was breathing pretty hard by the time he reached her, so he must have run a long way. 'I told Elliott I'd look after her, but I thought he was going to end up having to rescue her too when she ran off.'

'What do you mean, *rescue her too*?' Even hearing Elliott's name hurt.

'I was in the lifeboat station, getting a few promotional shots to use on Instagram, when they got a callout. Elliott had come down for an early morning training session before his new guests arrived, and he'd brought Splash down with him. He asked if I could look after the dog until he got back from the callout. I thought I'd better take her for a walk, but then she ran off in this direction and didn't stop until she saw you.'

'What was the callout for?' Anna had

that sense of foreboding again, like something bad was just waiting to happen. She'd never been this pessimistic before she lost Finn and she hated it.

'Some kid has disappeared from one of the holiday cottages.'

'Oh no, you don't think he's been snatched, do you?' Anna's hand went to her mouth, the thought of something like that happening in Port Kara was impossible to believe.

'No. According to his parents, he was convinced about there being buried treasure on the beach, and he couldn't wait to come back out again today to find it. When they called him and his sister down to breakfast in their holiday cottage this morning, she told them he'd gone out before it was even light and that he was going to get the treasure before someone else found it.'

'They must be terrified.' Anna couldn't even begin to imagine what the boy's poor parents were going through.

'They've had a search party combing the beach, but when they didn't find him, they decided to send out the lifeboat.'

'Is there anything we can do?' Anna tried not to picture what might have happened to the boy if he'd got into the water. Elliott was going out to face that, though, when he knew there was a chance he could encounter any person's worst nightmare. But that was Elliott, and it was a big part of why she loved him, even more than she'd loved Finn. She hadn't completely admitted it to herself until that moment, but she suddenly wanted Elliott to know it, too, more than anything. Except she'd ruined it, and now he hated her. If there'd ever been a chance for them, she'd blown it in the most spectacular way possible.

'They've got search and rescue teams going back over the beach and the cliff-tops.' Jasper shrugged, as if he wished he could do more, too. 'Why don't you go back and wait at the lifeboat station? I know Elliott will be happy to see you when he gets there. He'll need you, especially if the outcome is what we're all dreading.'

'He can't stand the sight of me.' She looked up at him. 'I told him what you said about him being a stepping stone, until I found someone I could love again, and I told him that I was leaving now because I was ready to move on.'

'You idiot, what did you do that for?' Jasper's words might have been blunt, but his tone was gentle.

'Because I fell in love with him. He was never going to be a stepping stone and you *knew* it!' The realisation hit her as she looked at him again.

'Of course I bloody did! I was just waiting for you to realise that he was the person you were supposed to fall in love with. If I'd told you that at the start, you'd have run a mile and had nothing else to do with him.'

'And that would have hurt me less, in the end.' Part of her wanted to slap Jasper for setting her up like that, but all the fight had left her body.

'Love hurts and life can hurt,

especially when you lose someone you love. But do you know what's worse than all of that?' She shook her head wordlessly, in response to the question. 'What's worse than all of that is not letting yourself love anyone just to try and protect yourself from getting hurt. If you live your life like that, Anna, then you might as well be dead already.'

'And you only get one life.' It was almost as if she could hear Finn whispering in her ear as she spoke.

'Finn wasn't right about everything, but he was right about that, and it would be a crime if you wasted your life hiding out from all the wonderful things you could experience, just because they aren't risk-free.'

'But what if that means my feelings for Elliott end up even stronger than they were for Finn?' The guilt was back again, washing over her like the waves on the incoming tide.

'Then great.' Jasper put a hand on her shoulder. 'Finn loved you, and you would probably have gone the distance, but Finn loved himself more.'

'You can't say that!'

'I can, because it's a trait I recognise in myself. Elliott's different and I could see the two of you were made for each other from the moment I met him. You just needed a little push.'

'But what if it's too late, after everything I said — '

'Just get over there. Take Splash back to the lifeboat station and say I gave her to you after something came up. It'll be the perfect excuse.'

'Thanks Jasper. You're a good man, even if you do try to hide it sometimes.' She leant forward and kissed him on the cheek.

'I didn't think I'd ever hear you say that after what happened with Finn.'

'Me neither, but things change.' She called back to him, already heading across the sand towards the lifeboat station. Life was too short to hold a grudge and it was too short not to take at least one risk. She couldn't leave without telling Elliott how she felt, and, if he felt the same, she wouldn't be leaving at all.

★   ★   ★

The lifeboat lurched as it hit another wave and Elliott gritted his teeth. The tide was coming in fast now and the wind was picking up, white horses dancing on the waves as the sky started to darken. It had been a glorious summer and, apart from the storm on the day they'd gone to Finbar Bay, the sky had seemed to be permanently blue and cloudless. Now there was a little boy lost somewhere, and if he'd got into the sea, just as the weather was changing for the worse, the chance of him surviving was next to nothing. The thought just piled on the misery that Elliott was already feeling, and he gripped on to the side of the boat as it rose up and down with another big wave.

'I don't think he's out here, do you? At least not anywhere we can see him.' Elliott turned to Jonty, the lifeboat

271

helmsman, whose face looked almost as grey as the sea.

'No, I think we should head back in and let the air sea rescue helicopter scan the area, it's the best chance of us finding him if he's out here.' Jonty shook his head, an unspoken understanding passing between them. If the helicopter spotted the boy, whose name was Noah Hampshire, it almost certainly wouldn't be a happy ending. 'We could be out here for hours otherwise and it might be better if we joined the search and rescue team on the beach instead.'

'I just hope that's where he is.' Elliott wanted to get back and join in the search as much as Jonty and the others did, but he didn't want to be on the beach when Anna headed off from Myrtle Cottage for the last time. She'd have to leave soon, though; the tide was heading in and the way out from the cottage by car would be cut off altogether by lunch time, until the tide went out again.

'We'll find him. I know this is cutting you up, but one way or another we'll bring Noah home to his parents.' Jonty clapped Elliott on the back.

'I know.' Elliott nodded. Jonty didn't need to hear that Noah wasn't the only thing on his mind. His problems were tiny in comparison to what the boy's parents were going through, but that didn't stop the thought of Anna leaving feeling like it was ripping out his heart.

* * *

Anna almost broke into a run as she got within sight of the lifeboat station. She was so close and not even the thought of having to admit to Elliott how she really felt, and why she'd said those awful things to him, could put her off. She was almost level with the network of caves that hollowed out the cliffs underneath Dagger's Head, when Splash suddenly jerked violently to the right and slipped out of her lead. Anna threw herself forward to try and catch the little dog, but Splash was too quick and, within seconds, she'd disappeared into the caves.

'Oh for heaven's sake!' Anna was beginning to wonder if Splash had preferred being a stray, she seemed so determined to escape at every opportunity. But if she didn't get her back, and soon, there was a real danger that the incoming tide would fill up the cave and Splash might not survive her encounter with water this time around.

As Anna reached the mouth of the cave, Albie began to pull on his lead too, dragging her in before she had time to think about whether it was safe to do so. Trying to keep hold of him and clamber across the slippery dark grey rocks was almost impossible. He started barking as the rocks led upwards and deeper into the cave, and she had to decide whether to turn back. There was a tunnel on the left hand side, which she knew from talking to Elliott led into a network of other tunnels that had apparently been used by smugglers for hundreds of years. On the right hand side was a dead end, where the rocks were more jagged and vicious, but Albie seemed determined to go that way, his deep bark echoing off the walls.

'She can't be up there.' Anna tried to tug him in the other direction. If the worst came to the worst, at least if they were in the tunnel they could keep climbing and stay out of the water. Eventually, the other end of the tunnel would open out to a crevice in a patch of woodland on the clifftop. It was a treacherous climb by all accounts, but at least they wouldn't drown. And if they couldn't make it to the top, they could at least wait it out until the tide went back out. If they took the dead end on the right, they'd be completely cut off by the tide. Only a complete idiot would risk that.

Suddenly, there was a far more high-pitched bark coming from the dead end on the right-hand side of where they were standing, and all attempts to persuade Albie into the tunnel on the left were off. He pulled away from her, his lead slipping out of her hand, and she had no choice but to clamber up the rocks and follow him towards where Splash had obviously gone. If that made her an idiot, then that's what she was. But, when it came to it, she couldn't leave Albie or Splash, even if it meant taking the biggest risk she'd ever taken. She had cuts all over her hands and legs by the time she reached the ledge that Albie had stopped on.

Peering into the darkness beyond the ledge, she spotted some movement. It had to be Splash. At least she hoped it was; if there was something else in there, she wasn't sure she wanted to know. Not that she believed in the local legends about witches and the ghosts of long-dead smugglers, but she was terrified enough as it was by the prospect of not being able to get out of the cave again.

'Come on, Splash, don't be scared.' Anna could hear the desperation in her own voice, so it probably wouldn't do anything to reassure the dog. 'Here girl, come on.'

'She's shivering; I think she's really

frightened.' Anna nearly lost her footing as she stepped back in disbelief. Whoever owned the voice sounded young, very young, and pretty terrified himself. She was so shocked that it took her a few seconds to realise it must be the missing boy, who Elliott was out searching for. She wished Jasper had known the boy's name, it would make this next bit much easier.

'I'm sure she's frightened. I'm just glad you're there to look after her. My name's Anna, and her name is Splash, I've got my dog, Albie, here as well.'

'I'm Noah.' His voice shook as he said his name. 'And I'm scared too.'

'It'll be okay, Noah. I promise. I'm going to get you and Splash out of here. Are you hurt?'

'I don't think so. I've cut my legs, but I think I'm okay.'

'That's good, Noah. How did you get up here?' It was a stupid question — there was only one way he could have got up there, but what she really wanted to know was *why*.

'I wanted to look for the treasure and I thought it would be in the cave, but then I got too scared to climb down again.' Noah started to sniff, finally giving into the tears that he'd obviously been holding in. 'I'm going to be in so much trouble.'

'No you won't, sweetheart.' Anna fought to keep her own voice steady. 'Everyone just wants to make sure you're safe.'

'Some men came and they were shouting my name, but I was too scared to answer them as well.'

'Don't worry, I'm here now and I promise I'm not scary. Albie really wants to meet you, too. He's Splash's best friend.' Anna felt in her jeans pocket. Thank goodness her mobile was still there. Once it illuminated, it was obvious there was no signal, but at least she could use the torch. Pointing it forward, she could see the narrow ledge that led to a wide platform where Splash was sitting on Noah's lap. He had tousled brown hair and a face so pale that he could easily have played the part of a ghostly smuggler. 'Do you want me to come up to you, or do you want to come back to me, if I shine the torch on to the ledge?'

'I'll come to you. I don't want us both to get stuck here.' Noah's voice had a new determination and he lifted Splash off his lap, standing up slowly.

'When you get to the edge of the ledge, I'll throw the end of one of the dog leads towards you and you can tie that around your wrist, so that there's no way you can fall.' Anna waited as Noah and Splash made their way to the edge of the narrowest part of the ledge. Splash trotted across towards her, as sure-footed as if she was just running across the sand, and Noah looked straight at Anna.

'I'm still scared.'

'I promise I won't let anything happen to you.' Anna forced herself to smile, hoping she didn't look as much like a shop mannequin as she felt. 'Okay, catch hold of the other end of the lead when I throw it over.'

It took three attempts before Noah finally managed to catch the end of the lead. Thankfully, Splash's lead was the type that combined a collar and automatically tightened to fit when you pulled on it. So all Noah had to do was slip the end over his wrist.

'I've done it. I'm ready.' The young boy nodded, his face already strained with concentration.

'Well done, sweetheart. Just take it really slowly and steadily. There's no rush.' Anna held her breath, almost as tightly as she was gripping the other end of the lead. His foot slipped when he was about three feet away from her, but he righted himself at the same time as she reached out to grab him and pulled him into her arms, both of them falling back on to the rocks behind her.

'I'm sorry.' Noah really started to sob and she was terrified he'd hurt himself in the fall.

'Are you okay, sweetheart?'

'Y-y-yes.' He got the word out

eventually and for a moment she just held on to him. Both dogs nudged them, making their own attempt to reassure Noah and Anna that everything would be okay.

'You did so brilliantly getting back across here. All we've got to do now is get back down to the bottom of the cave and then we can go and find your mum and dad.'

'You promise they won't be mad at me?' Noah looked up at her and smiled, this time for real.

'They'll be so happy to see you, nothing else will matter. Come on then, let's get back down to the beach.'

They picked their way steadily down the rocks, with Anna leading the way and holding out her hand to help Noah down when he needed it. Both the dogs were off their leads now; they were much more able to navigate the slippery rocks, and the even more dangerous gaps between them, than Noah and Anna were. But eventually they got to a flatter part of the cave. It was obvious then that the water level was rising. The dogs had stopped moving, and, when Anna stepped down again, she was immediately thigh-high in water. This time it was Noah who held out a hand and pulled her back up out of the water.

'What are we going to do now?'

'We're going to wait here until someone comes and helps us get out, or until the tide goes out again. It'll be okay whatever happens, I promise.' Just as Anna made Noah yet another promise she wasn't sure she could keep, a huge fork of lightning lit up the sky. A storm was on its way and she had no idea just how high the water level might rise. They might have to climb up the rocks again to where they'd started, but it had been wet and slippery up there too; she had no idea how high the water might rise and whether there was anywhere that would be safe to wait the storm out. Noah didn't need to know that, though. All she could do now was keep him safe for as long as possible and try to stop him realising how terrified she felt.

'I'm glad you're here, Anna.' Noah leant up against her and she put her arm around his shoulder, watching the waves crashing onto the rocks below them.

'I'm glad I'm here too, Noah.' Hugging him towards her, she realised she meant it. Whatever the risk to her, she wanted to be there for Noah and, in that moment, she understood Elliott better than she ever had before. She just wished he was there too. There was no-one else she wanted. Not ever.

★   ★   ★

When they got back to the lifeboat station, Elliott was praying that the little boy who'd disappeared would have been found safe and well, but a call had come through on the radio just as they arrived back to say that there were still no positive sightings of the missing child. The tide had now come in all the way, and there was just a narrow half-moon of sand at the lifeboat station end of the beach, which allowed access to the coastal path. The stretch of beach that ran from Dagger's Head to Myrtle Cottage was now completely cut off by the tide.

'The search and rescue team are concentrating on the cliffs now.' Jonty came into the kit room as Elliott and the others were getting changed and ready to join in the land-based rescue efforts. 'They think they'd have found him by now, if he'd still been on the beach, and if he isn't somewhere on the cliffs — ' Jonty didn't need to finish the sentence.

Elliott took his mobile phone out of the locker to check whether any of the guides who were working with the search and rescue team had sent him a message. But there was only one message and it was from Anna.

✉ From Anna

I don't think you'll get this because there's no signal on my phone. I tried to call you and it wouldn't connect. But if they find my phone afterwards, I wanted you to be able to read this. I'm sorry Elliott for everything, I didn't mean what I said. I love you. More than I've ever loved anyone. I found Noah, but we're trapped in the cave at Dagger's Head. Both the dogs are with us. Please forgive me xxxx

'I know where they are.' Elliott dropped the phone onto the bench beside him, already starting to pull his kit back on. 'Anna's in the cave at Dagger's Head, with Noah, and they've been cut off by the tide. The way this storm is closing in, the water level could rise all the way to the top of the cave if we don't get there.'

'Your Anna?' Jonty's eyes widened, as Elliott nodded. She was his Anna, and he had to get to her. 'I'll alert the helicopter team; they might need to winch them to safety, but we'll relaunch the boat as soon as the crew's ready.'

The rest of the crew moved just as

quickly as Elliott, everyone caught up in the sense of urgency that had filled the room. A loud rumble of thunder as the boat sped down the launch was another reminder of just how bad things were. The waves were already twice as high as they had been when they'd got back to the lifeboat station, and the sky was almost black with rain that seemed to be driving horizontally as well as vertically. It was vicious weather.

Elliott couldn't have spoken to the others, even if he'd been able to hear what they were saying over the sound of the roaring sea. Leaning his back against the wall of the boat, he just kept praying that he'd reach Anna in time and have a chance to say all of the things he so badly wanted to say to her. The things he'd been holding back since the moment they'd met. He'd told himself that it was moving too fast, and that they didn't know each other well enough to believe they could have fallen in love — especially when the things he did know about her suggested they couldn't be more different. But love didn't have a timetable or follow a set of rules where matching people's interests could guarantee you the perfect relationship. You were just supposed to grab it with both hands and be thankful it had found you. He'd never shied away from taking a risk. So why had he done it when the stakes were at their highest?

'The cliff opening is just up ahead, but we're not going to be able to get the boat in all the way, not with the waves bringing on water the way they are.' Jonty was still having to shout to be heard. 'We should just wait here on standby in case the helicopter crew need us — they can winch them up.'

'I can't just sit here and wait, Jonty. Not when I know they're in there.'

'Elliott, you can't, it's too dangerous.' Even as he spoke, Jonty was pulling out a length of rope. They both knew that Elliott was going to do it anyway, so they might as well make it as safe as they could. The helicopter had been called out on another emergency, just before they'd relaunched the lifeboat, and there was no way of knowing how long it would take before they got there.

'If you get the boat as close to the mouth of the cave as you can, I'll go in, you can tether the rope to me and I'll bring them back one by one. If we wait for the helicopter, it could be too late.' Elliott was already tying the rope around his waist, as Jonty secured the other end to the boat.

'What if we wait five minutes?' He had to hand it to Jonty, he was giving it a shot, but Elliott shook his head.

'I'm sorry mate, I just can't wait.' He double-checked his life jacket and the one he was taking with him to bring Noah back to the boat. Anna would have to wait until he came back for her, unless the helicopter beat him to it.

'Good luck, buddy.' Jonty clapped his hand on Elliott's shoulder again as he passed him, and seconds later he was in the water. They'd managed to get the boat to the mouth of the cave, so it shouldn't have taken him long to swim in, but with waves crashing against the rocks and the wind making the tidal flow fight against itself, it was much more of a battle than it should have been. Eventually he made it inside the cave, out of the wind and lashing rain, and it got a bit easier to swim.

'Anna! Noah!' Shouting into the cave, his voice echoed off the walls and for a moment he didn't hear anything. Then he heard a voice that was like music to his ears.

'Elliott! We're up here.' Looking up, he could see them on a ledge, about three feet above where the water had risen to. Swimming over until he was directly below them, he called up again.

'I'm going to throw this life jacket up to you, Anna; I want you to put it on Noah and make sure it's properly secured. Then Noah's going to need to jump into the water, so I can get him out of here and back on to the boat. When I've done that, I'll come back for you.'

'Okay.' Anna didn't even question it

or ask how he'd found them. There was so much he wanted to tell her, and a million promises he wanted to make her, but now wasn't the time. The only promise he needed to fulfil right now was that he would come back for her.

Taking his arm back as far as he could, he threw the life jacket up and, for once, luck seemed to be on their side. Anna caught the jacket and he could just about hear her reassuring Noah as she fastened the ties around him and made sure he was ready to go into the water.

'Everything okay up there?'

'Noah's ready, but he's a bit scared. I've told him you'll look after him, Elliott, and that I trust you more than anyone I've ever met.'

'Anna's right. I promise I'll look after you, Noah. You just have to be a brave boy one more time and jump into the water when Anna tells you to.'

'I'm going to count to three.' Anna's tone was forceful. 'One, two, three . . . ' Almost before she'd got to the final number, there was a splash just a few feet away from Elliott. Swimming over, he could see the little boy's face more clearly, and he looked absolutely terrified.

'It's alright Noah, I'm here now and in a few more minutes we'll be back at the boat.'

'Anna pushed me, but I know she had to, or I'd never have jumped.'

'She was just helping you.' Elliott used the extra length of rope he'd left hanging loose and tied Noah to himself, so that there was no way they could be separated when they left the protection of the cave. Taking up the slack on the other end of the rope until it was tight, he yanked it hard three times to let Jonty know he was ready to be pulled in. The progress they made back to the boat was far quicker with the help of the crew and, within minutes, Noah had been lifted into the safety of the boat.

'Are you sure you can make it back?' Jonty had barely got the words out and passed another life jacket over the side before Elliott began to swim away from the boat in the direction of the cave again, without even answering. It was even harder this time, but the thought of getting Anna back to safety drove him on. When he got back to her, he called up again.

'I'm going to throw another life jacket up and then you just need to do what Noah did and jump in.'

'I can't.'

'Of course you can. I'm here and I won't let anything happen to you.' It was the same promise he'd made to Noah.

'I know, but I can't leave the dogs here.'

'I'll come back for them after I've made sure you're safely on the boat.'

'They'll never jump into the water willingly. I can't leave Albie here, or Splash. I'm sorry.'

'There's no point me arguing with you, is there?' His voice was getting tight from shouting and swallowing water as he powered through the waves to get to her and Noah.

'No, sorry.'

'Right, when I throw the life jacket up, put it on Albie as best you can and then push him in. I'll get him back to the boat and then I'll come back for you and Splash. She's light enough for you to hold in your arms.' It took two attempts for Anna to catch the life jacket this time and getting it on Albie proved more difficult than getting a life jacket on Noah, judging by the amount of reassurance she had to give the dog. Eventually, there was a loud splash and Elliott swam over to him. Albie wasn't nearly as compliant as Noah either, and struggled all the way back to the boat, trying to get away from Elliott as if he held him personally responsible for the predicament he'd found himself in. Even with the rest of the crew pulling on the rope to get them back to the boat, it was exhausting.

'The bloody dog?' Jonty was incredulous when he hauled Albie on to the boat.

'She wouldn't come without them.' Elliott's words were coming out in gasps, and he was desperately fighting to get his breathing back into some sort of a rhythm. 'I need another life jacket.'

'You can't go back again, mate, seriously. One of us will have to do it.' Jonty held out his arm to pull Elliott back into the boat, but he turned away towards the cave again.

'I'm not getting out, so just chuck me the life jacket. Please.'

'You're insane.' Despite his words, Jonty threw a life jacket and it landed just in front of him.

'It's got to be me that goes. Good throw by the way.' Maybe he was being stupid and risking both their lives, but he had to be the one to bring her back. He loved her and he didn't trust anyone else to fight as hard as he would to save her life. The burning sensation in his lungs was agony as he swam against the violent waves, but nothing would stop him whilst he still had breath in his body.

'I'm here.' Elliott called up again, his throat burning with the effort of so much shouting. The light that had illuminated the ledge where Anna had been standing had gone out.

'The battery on my phone has died.' Hearing her voice in the dark, relief flooded his body.

'It's about to get very wet in a minute, anyway. I don't think a bag of rice is going to be able to salvage it after this.'

'I sent you a message, but there was no signal.'

'I got it; that's how I found you. It must have picked up a signal briefly at some point.'

'I meant what I said: I'm sorry.'

'I know, but you don't need to worry about any of that now.' He wanted to tell her he loved her too, but it felt like he would be jinxing things if he did. If he didn't say the words to her now, they both had to get back to the boat safely so he could tell her how he felt. 'I'm going to throw a life jacket up again, but it's going to be hard, because I can't see you anymore. So I need you to sing.'

'You're joking.'

'I'm deadly serious.'

'But I can't hold a note!' Her words were accompanied by a slightly hysterical laugh.

'Don't worry, it's not the X Factor.' Elliott waited and then she suddenly started to sing.

'I'll be riding shotgun underneath the hot sun, feeling like a someone . . . ' As she sang the lyrics to the George Ezra hit, Elliott took aim, throwing the life jacket and waiting for her to shout that it had missed her by miles and she couldn't see it. He wasn't sure he'd be able to go and get another one and make it back to her; he could barely feel his arms and legs as it was.

'I've got it!' Anna sounded almost as euphoric as he felt.

'Brilliant, put it on and make sure it's secured and then jump in with Splash in your arms.' It felt like an eternity until she answered him.

'I'm ready.' She didn't wait for his answer, and then he heard the sound of her hitting the water. Any second he was actually going to be able to reach out and touch her.

'Where are you?'

'Just to your left, I think. But Splash isn't happy.'

Swimming towards the sound of her voice, they were almost face to face before he finally made out her shape in the dark.

'Do you think you can keep hold of her?' Elliott already had a hand looped through one of the straps on her life jacket. He wasn't going to let her go. He was never going to let her go again.

'I think so.'

'Good, I'll tie you to me. All you've got to do is hold on to Splash, then the crew will pull us all in.' Even Elliott's hands didn't seem to want to cooperate as he tied a final knot in the rope and pulled it in tight again, giving three last yanks to let the crew know they were ready to be pulled back in. Wrapping his arms around Anna and Splash, he felt some of the tension leave his spine as they began to be dragged in the direction of the boat.

Untying Anna and Splash when they finally reached the side of the lifeboat, Jonty and the others dragged them on board, and then hauled Elliott over the side just as a helicopter passed overhead.

'Are you okay?' Anna threw her arms around him as Splash tried to get in between them, licking his face.

'I am now.' He pulled her towards him, not caring what the rest of the crew made of their reunion. If he'd had enough breath left in his lungs, he'd have shouted what he said next against the howling wind, so that everyone could hear. 'I love you, too.'

'I've been such an idiot. I don't care about the fact that you take risks for a living, I just want to be with you for as long as we're given. Like you said, no one knows how long they've got anyway, and we'll make the most of every day. I love you more than I've ever loved anyone.'

'I'm not going anywhere, I've got too much to lose now.' Elliott hoped she'd heard him but, with the boat racing back to shore, he couldn't be certain. It didn't matter, though, they had the rest of their lives together, and he was going to tell her every day just how much she meant to him.

Epilogue

The flowers around the door outside the Sailor's Chapel, by the harbour in Port Kara, were just as Anna had imagined they'd be. The florist had promised to use the same wildflowers that grew on the cliffs where she'd first met Elliott, and in less than twenty-four hours she'd be walking through the arch on her father's arm and down the aisle to where Elliott would be waiting.

'It's hard to believe that this time last year we didn't even know each other's names.' Anna kept her hand in Elliott's as they stopped by the edge of the harbour, to take a last look at the chapel, before they went their separate ways and spent the night before the wedding apart.

'And now I can't imagine my life without you in it.' He stroked the side of her face, sending a shiver down her spine. She was never going to get bored of looking into those dark brown eyes of his, which always seemed to be smiling when he looked back at her.

'So you don't think we're too different to make it anymore?' She raised an eyebrow.

'I'm a risk taker, you know that.' He laughed, and she couldn't help thinking about when he'd asked her to marry him. It was the day after they'd rescued Noah from the cave below Dagger's Head. They'd sat up into the early hours, just talking, and he'd told her that he'd been worried that they were too different and that she'd never understand his way of life. But when he'd seen the risks she took to save the little boy, he'd realised that deep down they were alike in all the ways that mattered. They'd talked about Finn, and how guilty she'd felt about falling so hard for Elliott. And she'd told him that, ironically enough, it was Jasper who'd finally made her realise that it was okay to move on; even if that meant moving beyond what she'd felt for Finn to a whole new level.

It was three o'clock in the morning when he'd asked her to marry him and, as shocked as she was, she hadn't hesitated for a moment. It was a risk that they'd both been more than willing to take.

'Don't take any unnecessary chances tonight, though, will you?' Anna grinned. 'If Billy and the others take you out for a last night of freedom, you could end up tied to a lamppost with your eyebrows shaved off.'

'I don't need a last night of freedom; I can't wait for tomorrow.' Elliott couldn't seem to stop smiling.

'Neither can I. It'll be brilliant to see Noah again, too.' The little boy whose rescue had finally brought them together was going to be a ringbearer at the wedding, and even Albie and Splash were allowed into the chapel. The reception was being held in an open-sided marquee on the private beach below the adventure centre, and everyone they cared about was going to be there.

'I know you're probably fed up with hearing this, but I love you, Anna Turner.'

'I think I can put up with hearing it another million or so times, if you can put up with me saying it back?' She tilted her face up towards his, and he didn't need words to answer her. It had felt like they were made for each other from the first moment they'd kissed. Finn had been right. You only got one life, and Elliott was the person she wanted to spend hers with. She'd never been more certain of anything.

Other titles in the
Linford Romance Library:

HEARTS AND FLOWERS

Vivien Hampshire

Though her former partner is completely uninterested in his unborn child, heavily pregnant Jess can't wait to meet her new baby. However, she hadn't planned on going into early labour at the local garden centre! After baby Poppy arrives, the manager Ed visits the pair in hospital, and they strike up a friendship. Ed finds himself falling for Jess — but can't quite bring himself to tell her. Will the seeds of their chance encounter eventually blossom into love between them?

WHAT THE HEART WANTS

Suzanne Ross Jones

Alistair is looking for a very particular kind of wife: a country girl who would be happy to settle down to life on his farm in the small town of Shonasbrae. Bonnie, fresh from the city to open her first of many beauty salons, isn't looking for a husband and she certainly isn't accustomed to country life. With such conflicting goals, Alistair and Bonnie couldn't be less compatible. But romance doesn't always make sense, and incompatible as the two are, they don't seem to be able to stay apart . . .